Vadim Mesyats

A Guest in the Homeland: Selected Writings

by Vadim Mesyats

in Russian:

Calendar of the Rememberer (poems, 1992)
The Wind from the Candy Factory (novel, 1993)
When We are Cheerful and Light (short stories, 1994)
The Leap Day: Selected Poems (1996)
The Way to the Sea (poems, 1996)
An Anthology of Contemporary American Poetry
(edited, with Arkadii Dragomoshchenko, 1996)

in English:

A Guest in the Homeland: Selected Writings (1997)

Vadim Mesyats

A Guest in the Homeland: Selected Writings

Talisman House Publishers
Jersey City, New Jersey

Published by Talisman House, Publishers
129 Wayne Street
Jersey City, New Jersey 07302

Some of the translation of these poems and short stories have previously appeared in the following magazines and anthologies, to whose editors the author is grateful: *Exact Change*, *The New Freedoms: Contemporary Russian & American Poetry*, *Red Shift*, *Yellow Silk*, *New Voices In Poetry & Prose.*

The author gratefully acknowledges the assistance of the following in the prepartion of this book: Igor Arnold, Nadia Arndt-Ernestus, Anne Beylina, Alex Cigale, Edward Foster, Vladimir Gandelsman, Marianna Grigorieva, Andrey Gritsman, John High, Marianna L. Hodgdon, Alexander Kaluzhsky, Christine Kunhardt, Nathaniel Tarn, and Natasha Yetimoff. The author would also like to express his particular thanks to Zoë English and Daniel Renfrew.

Library of Congress Cataloging-in-Publication Data

Mesi͡at͡s, Vadim.
[Selections. English. 1997]
A guest in the homeland : selected writings / Vadim Mesyats.
p. cm.
ISBN 1-883689-46-5 (cloth : alk. paper). -- ISBN 1-883689-45-7 (pbk. : alk. paper)
1. Mesi͡at͡s, Vadim--Translations into English. I. Title.
PG3483.3.E77A2 1997
891.78'509--dc21 97-34069
CIP

for my parents, Nina and Gennady

Contents

Editor's note

A Guest in the Homeland brings together translations and adaptations by various writers and translators drawn to Vadim Mesyat's work over the past several years.

Fiction: Tanya Beylin prepared the literal versions of "Someone Wandering in the Forest," "On the Lookout" (with Cheryl White), "Thank You, Deanna Durbin," and "The Museum of Natural History." Katya Tolstikoff prepared the literal version of "A Time for Freedom and Order." Final versions were done by Zoë English and myself. She and I are also responsible for the final version of Mark Lipovetsky's introduction. The interview was translated by Tanya Beylin with Zoë English.

Poetry: Bruce McClelland translated "Legend of the Bitter Frost," "I'll say good-bye to every ship . . . ," and "Winter Park." Alexander Kalouzhsky prepared the literal version of "Algae;" the final version was done by Alex Cigale. Vadim Mesyats prepared the literal versions of the remaining poems. The final versions of "I am burying a cow . . ." and "They were bringing gifts . . ." were done by Simon Pettet; the final versions of "1991," "Autumn Rainbow," "The Delta," "Taboo of the Children's Room," "A Guest in the Homeland" were done by Samuel Kent.

—*Daniel Renfrew*

A Guest in the Homeland

Mark Lipovetsky

INTRODUCTION

Not long ago, during Kruschev's democratic warming, poetry readings filled stadiums. But things have changed, and poets in Russia are no longer identified with prophets. Literature in post-communist Russia has become such a private affair that the publication of new books has slowed to a trickle.

But Russia, for better or for worse, remains an astonishing place. Faced with the kind of conditions a Russian writer has to deal with now, where else would a successful physicist who had received his Ph.D at twenty-five and was employed by one of the leading research institutions in the country suddenly abandon his career—in order to commit himself to writing?

Why not do as one might elsewhere and combine literature with one's main occupation? Because in spite of all the social and cultural changes, the Russian poet is still expected to dedicate himself fully to his task. For those who grow up surrounded by Russian culture, poetry can never be a mere hobby. It is a full-time commitment.

Mesyats' poetry, despite its apparently complex formal attributes, evokes memories of the old Russian tradition: "teary," one might say, or sentimental. This tendency is clear in traditional Russian romance and folks ballad, although it has been considered somewhat too naive for "serious poetry." Mesyats belongs to this tradition—he sings his favorite poems, for example, in a strange archaic manner, not with "music" in the conventional sense, but marking the rhythms with his hands. Reviving sentimental intonations and melodies, he is not afraid of being called primitive; rather, he tries to find a place for these seemingly timeless matters in a strict postmodernist context.

He doesn't avoid tears—his own or his readers'. Although raised in a major city, he is sympathetic to the world of the Russian fairy tale where nothing is insignificant, where a secret sense is hidden in every detail, and where EVERYTHING DESERVES COMPASSION.

What happens in a postmodernist context to sentimental values like sympathy, compassion and pity? To put it simply: why do we need them and what do they contribute to a contemporary artistic sensibility? It is easy to find those who will argue that the writer should remind society about simple moral values of the past. But this is a very dull and problematic explanation.

In his poems, Mesyats combines sentimentality with the strict rationality of Brodsky's intonations and cast of mind. His poetry involves a dialogue with Brodsky, but doesn't imitate him. The postmodernist context in Russian poetry was set out by Brodsky, and anyone trying to find his own place in that context will unavoidably engage in a dialogue with Brodsky's poetry and poetics.

Following Brodsky, Mesyats soberly recognizes (in Bruce McClelland's translation) "the world, always written in prose,/ In blissful ignorance continued to grow/ and/ If the soul is an illusion,/ the leaving of the body Would still be true for all times to come." In other words, no one can resist the disintegration and emptiness that envelops everything. In his short story "The Museum of Natural History," the world appears to be a great cemetery of bones, the grand finale of evolution, where a man's only decent attitude is to accept himself as one of the artifacts of this sad museum, to try to fit into the primeval scene without trying to change its wholeness. The scene reflects the completion of the history of human effort to change the world. For the physicist, the organic death of the universe has already occurred.

This, by the way, explains why so often in Mesyat's poetry and prose we encounter the theme of a bone-chilling cold. The Siberian cold is the direct result of the experiments with the revolutions and utopias: "The new age swept by like a snowstorm, / Carrying away millions in its wake," as Mesyats says in McClelland's translation. But this cold—and Siberia—appears to Mesyats as the only home given to him by fate, as the ground that harbors the roots of his soul. In the sentimentalist's tradition, home is an unconditional sanctuary. For Mesyats, it is one of the main dilemmas. His main characters are constantly in an oxymoronic position: a Guest in the Homeland. A tartar boy from the story "Someone Wandering in the Forest," losing his way in the dangerous winter forest, recognizes in a bird he finds his own father—the father that he never saw. Something similar happens with the narrator in "A Time for Freedom and Order," who describes his neighbor Lazarev, an old Soviet confused by myths. A former cook in a concentration camp, Lazarev tragically and comically suffers all the pitfalls of the perestroika era. The narrator's detached curiosity doesn't last long: by the end of the story, he finds something painfully familiar in Lazarev: "It has become absolutely clear that a person's past is the right place for freedom and order. The time when everyone can put everything the way he or she likes. Everything depends on one's mood and aims. So Lazarev and I keep smiling . . . because we know what freedom and order are. Lazarev and I. We are idealists" (translation by Katya Tolstikoff and Daniel Renfrew).

This bizarre form of idealism, emerging from an inability to deal with the entropy of the present, puts value only on the "forever lost." Following the logic of Mesyats' idealists, the main principle underlying the way things work is the principle of loss. Nothing will be saved, everything will perish.

Mesyats believes that only after having, so to sreak, shed tears for loss is it possible to acquire true knowledge of the value and meaning of a life consisting entirely of loss. Only after losing one's home, homeland, love, and even oneself can one finally take all of it back. An old Russian saying states, "We don't value what we have but cry when we lose it." Mesyats draws a paradoxical conclusion out of this trivial truth: it means, that to lose and to cry are essential.

I'll say good-bye to every ship,
and the birds heading south,
and every girl I love:
I'll just have to let them go.
(translation by Bruce Mc Clelland)

It is characteristic of the Russian sentimental tradition to explore the position of the "traveler," one who understands that the world, despite all its differences, contains the same simple and eternal feelings. Mesyats turns this traditional role into a philosophical formula:

You must come to prefer simple deceit,
And consider the pillage of foreign shores your own,

And thus become unfaithful to the City and the Globe.[1]
(translation by Bruce McClelland)

Losing his home, the Russian traveler in Mesyats' work feels at home under any streetlight. In the end, this sentimentality creates a purely postmodernist effect of presence/absence—a feeling of emptiness, a yawning open wound that turns out to be the only form of self-definition, the form through which one acquires a self-identity.

Another constant theme in Mesyats, purity, also springs from the sentimentalist's vocabulary. The word assumes an unexpected meaning for Mesyats, however: an openness to the winds, the readiness to lose and to cry, and to find freedom through it:

Getting used to unsteadiness as to the prevailing motion
could be hardly regarded as science,
but in the wind
it's perceived as a way to purity.

As if your pitiful contour is
being cut out of the cardboard of fabulous buildings
(translation by Alexander Kaluzhsky)

It is not the world that takes away everything one values; it is the self that gives the world everything in order to realize whether the things one values are really all that important, whether one's heart would or would not feel the pain of their loss. Strangely enough, in building his post-sentimentalist philosophy and ethics, Mesyats becomes one of the most relaxed poets of the new generation.

Mesyats has found a way to accept the world not in spite of its cruelty but because of it. It is because of the cruelty of the modern world that the way of loss is always open to mankind—and offers, therefore, a means through which to acquire the world and self-identity. While this may sound

[1] i.e. Rome, the "obs et urbis"

like masochism, it is a very commonplace, sentimental masochism—absolutely pure and inspired.

In reality, Mesyats occupies a childlike position: the child only notices his toy when it is not there for him. But perhaps this is the role of the sentimentalist impulse in a postmodernism age—returning the culture, paralyzed by the realization of its old age, to a state of childhood—a state before knowledge, and therefore a state of irresponsibility to everything past and present. The right to the loss defended by Mesyats is at the same time a right to irresponsibility, a right to forgetfulness: in Bruce McClelland's translation, "It's lucky I can remember that, since /Everything else is gone."

1991

More depressing than a dusty fishbowl in the reform school . . .
More absurd than a bookmark on the first page . . .
More mysterious than an old globe which in the twilight
Glimmers as always with the only Capital in the world.

More piercing than the shriek of drunken gulls
Flying in a wild bunch up over Sunday streamers,
Carrying hundreds of tragic faces down the black river,
Those by the round windows, lost in a deep sleep.

More colorful than a pile of lace lingerie ready for washing,
Rinsing expensive slips in a soapy water,
Suddenly getting embarrassed by a crazy fantasy:
Now you are living with all of the butterflies in China.

More luxurious than words that should be stated directly,
Even if they are both stupid and vain.
At least to get to a strange and distant continent.
Skimming over the steel turnstiles of Soviet Customs.

Quieter than a crumpled glove falling from your hand,
Hoping to rest in a safe place,
Rolling somewhere beneath a bench under worn-out heels,
No longer a continuation of anybody's gesture.

Scarier than the sound of a key turning in a rusty lock
And this is not my house?
More annoying than "Come on now, don't whine!" spoken by a friend,
This being more typical of him.

The whole year is like arguing with the Rainman
Whom first you curse, but then make up with.
He barely glances back, staggers away,
You will never really love until you leave.

And this is better than the people's dreams
Which are lost in some weird voiceless suspension.
When left alone amidst the emptiness
They come to nothing.
They are no longer distinguishable from the rest.

SOMEONE WANDERING IN THE FOREST

The Tatar children slide down the bright glittering slopes to the river. They sprawl on their wooden sleds, some covered with cloth, some not, and fly into the valley with their little arms outstretched as if they were planes. The slopes are bright with the kind of clothes children from the villages wear. From a distance it looks like flocks of disheveled sparrows braving the first rays of spring.

The children rush in all directions, picking on each other, standing together in groups, then wandering off by themselves. The clear blue sky means little to them—it is just such fun to be down here on earth. The sleds come to a stop at the bottom of the hill just as they reach the meadows. Those ridden by daredevils often flip over, sending their occupants head over heels or stumbling over some knoll or stump. Only the most prudent or luckiest get as far as the riverbank, leaving the rest far behind.

One of these, finding himself very close to the river's edge, looks back at his friends on the top of the hill. Too lazy to go back, he wipes his wet nose on his sleeve and heads for the river, struggling through slippery willow brushwood. He goes out to the ice and moves across the river dragging his sled. A thick crust of snow and ice supports him as he walks along, and inspired by the ease with which he moves, he heads for a place he's never been .

The forest.

A cleared path in a pine woods appears directly across on the far bank where the river curves toward a worker's town. The boy heard straight for the opening, where it will be easier to walk than through the thick trees and snowdrifts. For the last time he looks back at the hills and the children playing there. Nothing has changed during his absence. He moves on without doubt or regret.

He crosses some low, uneven hummocks broken by banks of snow and comes to the edge of the forest. Tall pines creak and groan like masts. The Tartar boy looks up, his hat firmly tied to his head. The huge trees do not scare him, though this is the first time he has seen them so close. The narrow path curves through the trees and snowdrifts. He goes deep into the dim, Christmas-smelling forest, moving so confidently and instinctively that the forest accepts him as someone who naturally belongs there.

No bird flies up from the trees, no wolf changes its course, smelling this approaching human; he is neither danger nor prey. But of course he is not a man yet, this little Tartar boy. The animals no doubt accept him as one of themselves because of his fur clothes, the natural milky smell of his body, and the fact that he is smaller than most creatures living in the woods. They sense that the boy cannot be aggressive, that he is going somewhere only because he is not cold yet, and that the curiosity leading him on is as familiar to them as their own.

The snow near the trees is melted and sunken, covered with pinecones and tiny pieces of bark. Snow here lasts a long time, clutched by the rapacious claws of the trees. Sunbeams reach the ground only after passing through the blue roof of branches and being diffused evenly through the air. This ideal tranquillity is seldom disturbed, and then only by the sound of a falling cone or sigh of a dying tree. The boy moves forward in this soft daylight, and it is only his sled with its seat made of yellow wooden slats that doesn't seem to belong, to fit in with the winter's monotony. He continues to drag it and sometimes it bumps the heels of his fur boots. Anyone watching him now would think the boy was pursuing some strange errand known only to himself or his employer. He walks easily, as if positive that somewhere in the wilderness somebody is expecting him. He cannot imagine they won't eventually find each other.

For a while the Tartar boy forgets his home and family and his many friends. He enjoys walking through the snow, around the bushes and stumps; it is so exciting here, much more fun than sledding with other children on the hill. He seems to know which way to go, how to avoid a dark ravine bristling with the dry twigs of fallen trees. Reaching a slope, he lies down on the sled (no difficulty doing that) and speeds down the hill, turning his high cheekbones into the wind.

After another fast descent, he proudly looks around. He doesn't fully realize he is all alone and nobody can see him. He has covered a great distance. It no longer matters that there's no one around to compete with. Who but himself would care that he slid so far? He is about to retrace his steps to the to the top of the hill when suddenly he discovers his path again.

This time the trail follows a thawed patch of snow where he can clearly make out the fresh oblong tracks of some unknown four-footed animal. Excited to find something new, the boy tries stepping into the clawprints. He follows the path down into a glen bathed in the afternoon sun. Sometimes it runs up against shapeless masses of rotten leaves and root stubs. The boy remembers how he once saw such leaves in the fall when there was no snow around. He winces, noticing a black steamy clod of dung; Sonka, their timid old spotted cow must be rambling nearby. He can almost hear the dull scraping of the cow's bell. And although there is actually no sound at all, the silence does not disturb or worry him.

The iron runners of his sled rustle as he pulls it along, and the snow squeaks under his fur boots. Still cheerful, not realizing the gravity of his situation, he goes deeper into the enchanted woods. He finds himself in a dense crowd of trees growing very close to each other and stands for a long time under a broken mountain ash, instinctively tearing off clusters of withered berries that have miraculously survived since the spring and cramming them into his mouth.

All of a sudden, he feels a wild and concentrated gaze from behind the trees. It's an eagle owl. Appearing out of nowhere in the middle of the day, the great bird perches low to the ground, its talons clutching a truncated bough. Drowsy, awakened by the unusual spring warmth, it stares gravely and vacantly at the boy. The boy himself, feeling as if he has suddenly become even smaller than he is, gazes back directly into the bird's eyes, still furtively swallowing the overripe berries.

The boy doesn't know quite what he is looking at and why it sits there so close, obliterating the rest of the world from the young traveler's gaze. Huge, sitting so woodenly and unmoving, the owl makes no response to the weird tattered creature, nor does it close its eyes again, perhaps thinking it too early to drift back to sleep. The boy cannot decide what to think about such an unusual spectacle. Who on earth can this be, peering so intently at him and his sled? He shifts from foot to foot, breathing quickly, his mouth smeared with juice from the berries. And suddenly struck by a surprising, unexpected idea, he says to himself, *This is my father. . . . That's him, really him. . . . He's always watching me. . . . And that's him right now. . . . So close. . . .*

He repeats this to himself again and again. It may be nonsense, but something in it is deeply healing, too. Choking with his first real tears of loneliness and happiness, he does not hear the bird's frightened jerk as it flies from its branch, nor does he see the shadow as the owl shoots up into the darkening skies, flying away over the evergreen forests south of the tundra, over the hills and plains, to the North, the solitude, the deserted gulags of the Komi Republic.

ON THE LOOKOUT

I was brought to that mysterious apartment several times before along a wide shining road, with trees on either side. Those who brought me answered my endless questions carefully and indifferently. Then I was left alone behind the closed door to guard the old clocks, the ruined sewing machine, or my grandfather's staff with its handle shaped like the muzzle of a dog with his teeth bared. My grandfather always took with him various metallic gadgets that clicked and banged against each other, jutting out of his string bag with sharp parts that caught on my clothes. I stood there among them like a jack-in-the-box, leaning on the staff and looking down on the glimmering, icy incrustations at the bottom of the frozen stairwell.

The door, massive and eternal, moved easily on its hinges until the tiny lock clicked shut. The lock obviously didn't belong there. It looked more designed for some ancient religious book than for a stronghold of peaceful, domestic human life. Silence might well reign behind that door. Or heavenly voices of young women might be heard. Perhaps gloomy old men sat there on trunks held together with strips of brass. Or perhaps the house was totally empty, or exotic flowers coiled around the solid bars of cages as they might in the menagerie of some Asian tzar.

After the door clicked shut, a tiring sweetness made your head go round, and you felt hot and sick. All you wanted to do was undress, kick off those boots that were a little too big for you, tear off the suspenders stretched across your chest, and drop the belt with the scratched military buckle onto the floor, together with the stupid childish hood, the overcoat, the cap, and all the rest, until you finally emerged from the pile of phony clothes feeling fresh and even more alive in the sudden winter coldness that crept up the sooty stairwell.

I was not as little then as they thought. I asked about one thing but remembered another; my curiosity was only a way to communicate with those who wanted me to speak. Yet alone, guarding my grandfather's bags, I never uttered a peep or tried to discover details about the forbidden lives of the people I saw on the landing. They would come up to me, stroke my round fur hat, then mumble something in surprise when they saw a cuckoo bird awaken in this or that clock. I never answered them, though I felt their kindness in those agile, medical fingers studying my head. I knew that these polite men and women would soon go away. I worried that I might be left there for a long time, maybe for my whole life. I never knew when my grandfather would be back and we could move into that unhealthy, yellow light of the streetlamps, which I hated even more than my loneliness.

One time we approached the house in the early evening, though somewhere deep in the trees and empty verandahs it was already night. Suddenly I felt that all those lights had originated not inside this mansion but from some huge, aging face that could reveal everything yet unknown to me: wisdom . . . and beauty . . . and the bitterness of inevitable but justified tears . . . and love . . . and the forgiveness for lies. We moved slowly, feeling the power and attraction of those rich, unflickering flames, and I clearly saw that my grandfather's features had smoothed. No emotion showed in them butthe overwhelming oblivion experienced only in the cradle.

Our everyday life was somewhere far behind us. I was enchanted by the new enveloping place that would soon belong to one of us, and I moved forward as if in a trance until I bumped into a hard leather apron covered with frozen drops of milk. Standing in front of me was a bulky, untidy man. His screwed up his lips silently as if to laugh silently. He was transporting heavy aluminum churns from a painted wooden sleigh down the stairs and into some low, dark cellar next to our mysterious house. The milk slapped back and forth inside the churns, hich swung wildly in his clumsy embrace. Just in passing, I thought—I don't know why—Aha, they have a milk depot here. I should remember this. We might need milk later.

Suddenly I grew keenly aware of what I hadn't wanted to see at all: my own little curved shadow with a walking stick. The projection of the dog's muzzle on its handle could be seen clearly against the snow. It was obvious that the two of us, my grandfather and I, having taken each other's hands, were following someone else, some guide.

He played cards there, in that house, that unpredictable old man. I came to know about it later, when I understood better the course of events accompanying our visits there.

The sleigh with our food usually came in the evening. It contained bony meat, bread wrapped in sacking, huge heads of cabbage, genuine Tartar cottage cheese. Empty boxes were returned on the same sleighe. All these tasks were performed by the same worker. He could not speak because of some disease but only mumbled, swinging his arms encased in the leather gauntlets. Once, when I was sitting on the windowsill looking around, I saw him standing in the yard, leaning his forehead against the horse's flank, which was covered with white frost. He didn't look as if he were thinking about anything. He was probably mumbling again in his thoughts, listening to the horse's stomach and the crack of snow under its hooves echoing somewhere inside its body.

My grandfather was acquainted with this man, though I didn't take part in their contacts. My grandpa would leave me with his mechanical gadgets and step aside, lightly embracing his terrible friend. I was sure they were hiccupping and mumbling secrets to each other. Why was I not to hear them? So I wouldn't get scared? They both ignored me purposefully, though that half-man might possibly have become the best intermediary for grandfather's and my mutual understanding.

We underestimate people with born intellectual defects. Their inner lives must offer them unique experiences rarely given to the rest of us. He had never said a word in his life. Neither had his mind created any strange language that could spawn into the beginning of knowledge. But nature on the other hand could not absolutely reject his animal soul. I believe that deep in that soul, day by day, glance after glance, some extraordinary, sinless, and of course human domain was being erected.

Another reason he did not become our mediator, as I see now, twenty years later, was his convulsive appearance. Even today, my most awful dream is of him turning over and over in puddles of milk in the frost near the stairs leading to our porch. This huge, mighty epileptic has selected me from all the rest of mankind. Surprised by anything small and ashamed of his own grandeur, he is full of hatred and shakes his head and quickly pouts his lips, rejecting the unnecessary help of his hospital attendants.

Fear was almost the only emotion living in me then, hiding somewhere in my chest. It seemed to wait for the end of the day, and become sold and perceptible when darkness fell. I was not afraid of the darkness. It was simply, like my fear, impenetrable and obscure, primordial, foolish,—having nothing in common with the feeling of intimidation that characterizes one's later experiences in life. That early fear belonged to me and nobody else. It resembled the desperation of dreams, emerging out of nothingness, out of the chaos that exists even before we come into being.

There I stood, face to face with my fear. The location of this loneliness was quite exact. It was the threshold, and to cross it required a single step, the step after which everything changes, even without our participation, and becomes obvious and constant, the place after which it can be seen that the man has found himself, and will always be what he is now: miserable or generous, sensitive or tough—exact, predictable, if we may speak so of human beings at all.

Perhaps I had sensed that to give in to the orders of the adults was necessary for my safety. I was protected, though for some reason I still tried to protect myself as much as possible. I didn't speak much, never eavesdropped, and hardly moved. I did the only thing permitted as much as I could: *I watched—I kept a lookout* Choosing to focus on only those things I wanted to, feeling no connection with what I saw, I remembered everything, each tiny detail, whether I wanted to or now, forever.

I entered the room quite casually. It had been terribly dull in the corridor. My grandfather had not appeared, and the neighbors with their garbage pails had disappeared, so there was no reason to guard the bags with the clocks. Moreover, with every new move of the many hour and minute hands, I became more and more certain that there was nobody behind the door. Either they had all left through the back or had simply never been there at all. At the least, this terrible guess proved that everything was prepared for my entry. The dangerous obstacles were removed. Cerberus was dead. The way was open.

The first thing I saw was a dog with its head turned in an unnatural way. A short tongue with pale dots hung out of the side of its muzzle. It was lying down, occupying almost the whole hall, and not moving, though I walked in circles around it. I'd say it was lifelessly thinking. (If something alive stopped all purposeful movement, in my childish imagination I'd feel it was peacefully thinking about its simple sorrows.) In the dog's rich, thick hair some small, wet and lively ball of a puppy was rolling over. The strange serenity of the dog passed into me and made me forget those surprising moans and guttural roars of suffering I had heard so often through the locked door. God knows what grown-ups do so busily to make their lives more eventful and interesting. So I delicately caressed the dog with the stick and, stepping over its bowl of soup, walked on, in silence.

My grandpa was sleeping in the rear room. His clothes hanging on the chairs were warm, as if they had just been taken off. The sunlight drifted through the windows, and in the overwhelming indifference and tranquillity, everything around me became understandable and simple. We had moved into a new house—would be living there—now this room belonged to me—my whole life was in front of me—I would have lunch very soon . . .

For a long time, other people lived in that house with us. They owned most of the furniture left in the rooms: the huge bookcases full of encyclopedias, the settees with musical squeaks, the grand piano with a cricket in it, the trunks swarming with moths. The main purpose of all these objects was to radiate light-sparkling dust, to let out golden mosquitoes, to strike me with the hard, dry smell of bygone days. The clocks and gramophones of my grandfather were not out of place in this dying household. I placed them on top of the cupboards, completely wound, and my fantastic town would ring out, beating the time discordantly, screaming with some crippled spring.

Now, many days later, in the days of another removal (so much like that old one) watching the permanent aging and decay of this house, which is never complete, I often come to a strange and fanciful conclusion. I think that smouldering away like this is something not limited to any particular time or stage in one's life, and the greatest courage of ordinary life is to accept this fact with humility. Anything eternal exists beyond and apart from our everyday work and the details of the world, then it must be absolutely indifferent to what we know and think, and visits us only casually, to soothe or to explain something . . . this story, for example. Sometimes it seems to me that I too can stop, let all the roads take their normal course, let time pass without affecting me. I can be the same as I am now, young and unknown, allowing myself the most perfect luxury: a life seeking nothing. We already have *everything*, a priori. I don't know why people admire restlessness, the nervousness of artistically gifted persons, sensing in them, if not holiness, at least their full accord with the world. Why is revelation supposed to offer the perfect bliss? Why is it acceptable not to trust anything truly indifferent, as if there were nothing to be revealed there except death?

Everything living feels it must rush about, striving for its goals, rejecting them, and returning again to the pursuit. But is this senseless passion, this desperate search—which is nothing but doubt—the notorious "labor of the soul" that should protect us from featureless denial? We all fuss around primarily for each other. If each person then joins a surrounding life which is strangely unfit for him, has he not then very little left of his own life?

Only in my childhood, in an age so near to oblivion, did fate bring me together with the one person congenial to me—my grandfather. In me, he was happily rejoined with his primordial dwelling, and in those parting days, when opposing elements were approaching us, we could answer all these innumerable questions. Perhaps that was exactly why we did not want to speak at all.

I am burying a cow
Mourning my sister
Upon a bank of nettles
With head bowed

Sister, oh sister
Meet with you soon in paradise
Pitching pebbles into the flames
Your white ribbons.

They were bringing gifts to his resting place
Birch bark baskets
Milk, that was heavier than stone
I was looking up at what were clearly wings
Saying—it seems to be getting light
Holding my head in my hands

The apparition of my mother in a white lace shawl
Singing and bending over me.

A TIME FOR FREEDOM AND ORDER

for my grandfather, Andrey Romanovitch

A neighbor of mine named Lazarev met Samoylenko, a lonely pensioner, in 1980. People from our community were planting trees around Lazarev's house, digging, hoeing and talking. It was late, but they didn't go home. "I'd like you to come and see me any time that's good for you," Lazarev said to Samoylenko. "Meet my wife," and added, "See you tomorrow." But for some reason, whatever it may have been, several days passed before Samoylenko turned up. He climbed to the upper floor, spread his handkerchief, and showed a gray iron medal. "Let me tell you about myself." And my neighbor Lazarev drew the curtain for the sake of decency, explaining as he did so, "The TV-screen will have a better picture." By the time they said good-bye, they were on friendly terms. They decided to see each other at their respective homes and share memories.

A look into the past is always very optimistic. The future is just a hope, something you think about every day. Idealists, especially if they are old, should prefer the past. The old men turned out to be unmitigated idealists. Lazarev had spent all his life working as a cook. He was a ploughman first and then became a cook. A long time ago his father, the head of the family, had come here from the Ukraine with other settlers. Lazarev's brothers (four, I think) were old enough to help their parents clear the land and root out stumps for planting. It was Lazarev's bad luck to be born on the way here. No one needed the child or wanted to take care of him. All day long he was left in a sort of dug-out or trough where worms stuck to his body. But he survived in spite of everyone's expectations to the contrary. At least that much is certain, as I can testify, having been his neighbor for ten years. He was the most remarkable person in our neighborhood. He wasn't a troublemaker. Even if he'd had a drink he could behave himself. I do not know what made him so attractive to everyone. He was a bad mixer.

Talking to a stranger seemed unpleasant to him. Even if were the one to open a conversation, he would become a bit aloof. And he was in the habit of wearing suitcoats and spent a lot of time looking in the mirror, combing his hair.

I believe he was about seventy when I gave him a green accordion. I knew that when he was young (a term that seemed rather elastic when applied to him) he had been able to play the accordion well and compose music. The accordion I gave him turned out not to be the one he needed. Its sound was different from the Russian kind he preferred. I was completely unaware such distinctions existed and had brought him something Western, I suppose. He didn't want to change his manner of playing so he set the instrument aside, but his attitude toward me changed for the better. In the end he sang me something very interesting of which I understood almost nothing, but the words "tin-tin-tin Martin" stuck in my memory. That part seemed tremendous. Very energetic.

When he spoke it was with great feeling, but his excitement lasted only a few minutes. Then he would shake his head and say "Never mind. It's really nothing."

"Please, go on . . . "

And then he would say again, loudly, "It's really nothing."

After that he would go on with his story or fly off on a tangent. And everything started over again. Lazarev spent a lot of time talking to Samoylenko and I couldn't understand why. He spent a lot of time not only talking but arguing. They had heated debates, I suppose. The trouble was t Lazarev's stories were all about the same things. He went over them adding unexpected details and then changed everything all over again. But the stories themselves were always the same. No matter how hard Lazarev tried to fool me, I'd managed to put everything together and restore the narrative in its original form in my imagination. Names, towns, events chained him to his memories. Lazarev's reminiscences included things he had mentioned earlier. It was, I felt, pointless to try to make him change the subject or ask him to talk about something else. I doubt if there was anything in his life aside from these stories:

The feud between the Khokhols[1] and the Chaldons[2] in Siberia. Stealing someone's bride. Living on the streets. The death of his children. His aunt's tuberculosis and the years spent with her when she was dying. His parents being stigmatized as kulaks.[3] Exiled like Montague and Capulet. Cooking at the mine. The young couple's wanderings. Searching for his banished father Roman, who became a rag-and-bone man on his return. Being arrested. The Baikal-Amur Railroad. Being attacked when he stood up for his rights. His friend Oreol's escape. The shtrafnaya colonna.[4] War. A letter to his wife with hopes for they could rendezvous at the Taiga station.The terrific disappointment when that didn't happen. Then living in the republic of Komi. Being a cook in a jail. Another family. Other children. Medals and other rewards. The Victory. His protest against having only methyl alcohol to drink to celebrate the end of the war. Released from jail. Desiring to see his children. Looking long and steadily through the window at the barber's where his wife caressed the cheeks of a miner Lazarev did not know. Returning to his family. Debauchery. His witty mind and experiences. Moving to a bigger town. His young neighbor's unnecessary present. That seemed to be the whole of it with the exception of certain details. That's really all.

All this added up to a pleasant, kind-hearted, intelligent man with white hair. Walking with him, one could talk about the Communist Party, the government, and divine predestination.

He also had a very special story about a cake with doves. That involved his good fortune once in being noticed and praised. In the early days of socialism, he baked that wonderful thing for one of Stakhanov's[5] famous followers, Aksenia. It was a merry surprise, fireworks at the dawn of socialism. A great number of office-bearers, including comrades Drobnis and Norkin, joined the party as specially invited guests. Lazarev wore a white

---

[1]Ukranians

[2]Cossacks, migrants from the Don River region in southern Russia

[3]affluent farmers, subject to repressions during collectivization

[4]or "penalty column," a section of the gulag concentration camp with especially severe regulations

[5]Aleksei Grigorievich Stakhanov was a miner whose productivity—reportedly fourteen times the average—was used by Stalin as a model to encourage workers.

cook's-cap for the festival. His cake had three pyramids, like those at Giza, with bright lemon frosting. People clapped when they saw it with the enthusiasm one would expect at meeting of the Party. Lazarev set the cake across from the famed Aksenia on a specially prepared stand, said "Congratulations," and with a magical wave of his hand opened the secret door and . . . Off they went! Off! The doves flew out of the cake straight into the faces of the dignitaries. A triumph! "Well, " he said, "I had covered the bottom with a sheet of buttered paper. I was afraid that they might spoil everything there. I had disguised them carefully. It was my best moment."

Samoylenko liked these stories. He had taken an active role in reconstructing the country and thought his contribution had been great. Thus, he would put on airs when dealing with others. He believed that an air of self-importance was necessary when dealing with others lest they misjudge him.

Samoylenko and Lazarev saw the New Year in together. Samoylenko brought pancakes wrapped in a newspaper. The old woman made pelmeny[1]. Lazarev made samogon[2]. They sat up late watching "Melodies and Rhythms" on TV. They tried to dance and eventually managed to. In the end, they quarreled. For no particular reason, Lazarev had started to talk about a great misfortune he'd had many years ago. He had been accused of "porazheniye"[3] under Clause 58 and spent fifteen years in jail. But in fact what he he had done was spend a night fucking the wife of an administrator. Samoylenko became very self-righteous and said that he himself would have imprisoned a scoundrel like his companion. Lazarev, as I later understood, almost couldn't distinguish between his private and his political acts. I was stunned by the fact that when interrogated he didn't confess a thing. That could only mean they had promised to kill him, but he didn't confess anything simply out of spite. He didn't expect any further sexual favors from that woman. He understood the administrator correctly. Even if he hadn't, he would have done the same thing twenty years later. He thought

---

[1]Russian ravioli
[2]homemade vodka
[3]i.e., counterrevolutionary activity

everything that had happened to him was a mistake of Comrade Yezhov's[1]. The administrator had been killed with an axe a year and a half later.

Lazarev had a copy of a book on the history of the Party written in Ukranian, and he tried his best to read and understand it, but the language of his ancestors was his weak point. He didn't laugh at this "history" as I did, and he never stood on ceremony with Samoylenko. That New Year's Eve, Samoylenko had barely finished confessing that he had been an informer than Lazarev pushed the table upside down. I don't think Lazarev actually cared much about such details. Certainly Samoylenko had boasted earlier that he had imprisoned ninety or so people at the match factory he worked for. I think Lazarev knew from the very start that Samoylenko had been a bastard, but at first they didn't fight. But this time Lazarev threw himself at Samoylenko trying to grab his throat with one hand (it was against the rules of good sportsmanship to use the other) but eventually fell asleep with his head resting on the table. Samoylenko was furious. storming about the room, throwing around his dentures and glasses. He left, muttering the offensive word "convict." And "convict" was indeed what Lazarev was, while Samoylenko himself was the "jailer."

He returned the next morning to get his denture back. He was invited to have something to eat.

"Join us. It's a holiday again. Cuba's Independence Day." They were showing Cuban dances on TV: black girls decorated with ostrich-plumes were dancing in a ring while their partners, thin and graceful, each rested on one knee and held big hats. "Hum!" Lazarev seemed to be in high spirits.

"How many days did you spend in action?" Lazarev asked. "I bet you crippled that arm yourself."

"You're wrong. The fascists picked on me deliberately."

"It's all very strange, isn't it—I mean that it was your arm that attracted them? They could have shot off something else as well."

"That's exactly what they did. While you—you rat—stayed in the rear." Samoylenko was holding his dentures high above his head.

---

[1]People's Commissar of Internal Affairs from 1936 to 1938.

"Well, come on, show me your medal. I don't remember exactly where they sell them."

"You ask where? At the Second Belorussian front. That's the answer."

"Are you a Belarussian then? Maybe a Belo-Pole[1]. Or do you mean the name of the station[2]?"

"You've got a religious surname."

"So do you."

Then the old woman gave the two men some wine to calm down. "Come on, stop quarreling. We're happy to see you again, Ivan Samsonovitch."

There was no need to ask Ivan Samsonovitch to drop in again. The two men couldn't do without each other. Utterly different though they were, they had become one.

Although he had a pension, Samoylenko worked as a mailman. The post office was just across the road. The old man didn't find it difficult to fetch the mail and distribute it in the apartment block where he lived.

"Fresh newspapers for the enemy of people[3]," Samoylenko said to Lazarev without malice.

"I would never have thought one of the oppressors would be serving me," Lazarev would respond.

One day Samoylenko arrived earlier than usual. He looked very solemn, a handkerchief peeping out of his coat pocket. "Wine is outlawed[4]. Now you can be sent to jail for drinking wine."

"I didn't ask you to have a drink. I don't want to share a cell with you."

"They won't even show wine on TV. Look at this article. It says we are being seduced. They want to make us a nation of drunkardss."

"Who are they?"

---

[1]Soviet name for Polish army units opposing the Red Army in the Revolution.
[2]The Belorussian Station is a railroad station in Moscow.
[3]or "vrag naroda"—the term for a person oppressed during Stalin's regime
[4]In 1986 during the partial prohibition introduced by Mikhail Gorbachev, there was a public campaign against drinking and reduced availability and sale of liquor.

"Enemies of the people. You, for example. You, Lazarev, making samogon secretly. I am going to turn you in. I'm going straight to the Central Committee. This is a very serious matter indeed."

Samoylenko was staring at the big jar of wine Lazarev kept in the kitchen. "A little drink? I can smell alcohol," he asked with hope in his voice.

"What the hell are you talking about? A little drink! It's got no yeast. No sugar. And then you'd go and turn me in. Let them come and check."

"Sure, but a jar like that arouses suspicion."

Once I found them standing in a line with me in front of the wine store. A person could buy wine only if he had a special coupon. The pensioners had to push through the crowd to get to the counter, and it upset me to see Samoylenko and Lazarev pushing each other along, using their rights as pensioners to be first and making their way against the crowd, roaring, punching, fighting . . .

Then free elections were announced. Samoylenko looked embarrassed when he brought the news. Lazarev was puzzled, too. "It's either a revolution or the Party's way of dealing with the way things are now," he said.

"I think it's a far-sighted decision," Samoylenko suddenly put in.

"We'll learn who is who very soon."

"I learned who you are long ago."

"Likewise."

They went together to the polls. They hid from each another in the voting-booths for a few minutes, obviously casting their ballots for one and the same candidate. They were strangely impressed by the secrecy of the procedure.

On their way home they gazed with horror at the walls covered with posters. They tried to avoid demonstrations and angry crowds. Neither of them dared to discuss the events, which seemed outrageous to them. Lazarev was not interested in who Samoylenko had voted for, nor did Samoylenko care whose name Lazarev had checked on the ballot. Both wanted simply to get to the kitchen and have some of the forbidden wine. And that's what they did. Then they watched the celebration of Cuba's Independence Day over and again, throwing their dentures at each other.

They spent their days in August silently drinking port.

"Wonderful music," said one, listening to the radio.

"Somebody must have died,"[1] said the other.

Then Lazarev told the story of the cake again. Samoylenko remembered that as a child, he had stolen his neighbor's bag of potatoes. "Shame upon you," said Lazarev. "You're a communist."

"I wasn't a communist that time," Samoylenko answered gloomly. "There were no communists then."

I happened to see them about this time. A great, splendid funeral procession was being shown on TV. "What are they burying?" I asked.

"Totalitarism," they answered. "Three idiots smashed by a tank. They were very totalitarian, Dimochka. Three warriors.[2] So sorry for their kids. Don't go out late at night."

Then the Party was abolished. Samoylenko brought this news to Lazarev together with a bottle of vodka. "The Party is abolished, but God and wine are are back. Tact is in fashion now, if you follow my drift."

Then their reminiscences got better of them them.

"Do you like Jewry?" Samoylenko asked suddenly.

"I do," answered Lazarev. "The main thing is that even they can be cheated. In the Far East I fooled an inspector's once. We knew he was going to arrive and I made my team work all night long. In the morning it took us three or four hours to get that work finished right before his very eyes. We had everything ready so the rails could be laid. He told the authorities how productive we were, and they started to feed us better. Those criminals took quite a fancy to me. That's all I know about Jewry. They say they have a nice cuisine." Samoylenko seemed ashamed about something. Lazarev seemed to feel that way, too.

Then the country was abolished. But the old men never noticed for they had fallen in love. Both had fallen in love with the same woman, their neighbor, a music teacher. She could be heard playing music on the other

---

[1]During the coup that August, only classical music was broadcast; news programs were cancelled, as they had been when political leaders like Brezhnev, died.

[2]a reference to the painting known as "The Bogayrs" by Victor Vasnetsov in the Tretyakov Gallery, Moscow.

side of wall. Even now everyone in our apartment block remembers her, for she could play better than anyone, and everyone got very excited about it. She was married, however, which was. of course, a problem for the old men. Once she came and asked if she could borrow a wrench. Lazarev had nothing but his wife, his sofa, his TV, and his pictures of the children. Samoylenko, however, said that he was the best plumber anyone had ever seen. He and the woman lived on the same floor, so he had already known her for a long time, and they went off to repair the pipes.

Lazarev was taken aback. He told the woman for no apparent reason that he could make wonderful mouse-traps, twirl springs on a nail easily, and wished all informers had been punished. Then he began tapping the pipes gently with scissors. It would be hard to say exactly he meant to challenge. The police arrived, but they were one looking for a group of drunk youngsters, and there was no harm done.

And so October passed. December passed. October came again. There was only one person in our neighborhood who earned a lot of money. That was me. I wanted to move to a new house. I could have bought Lazarev a pig, a cupboard, and hundreds of accordions with Russian sounds, but he would never have accepted them. It was not a question of pride; there was nothing he needed. He celebrated Cuba's Independence Day by tapping the radiator with with scissors .

Samoylenko stopped delivering newspapers to Lazarev, but he used to come to see him and talk. "What did they give you to eat? Did it look like soup? I've never tasted anything like that. How many guards did you have?"

I don't think the old men were interested in television, newspapers, and things like that. Samoylenko felt anything important that was going to happen would happen in his apartment. He didn't care for politics. They were idealists about the past, and the past was connected with modern reality somehow. They supported each other in this. They were ready to accept only cigarettes, wine and bread from the outside world.

When I dropped by their cozy place to supply them with the things they needed most I felt their warm hospitality. They looked like prisoners taking a parcel from children. Then Samoylenko learned how to play the Viennese accordion. That was the last time I saw my dear and lively neighbor dance. Decorated with garlands of medical tubes and bottles, with his belly twisting around, dressed in a coat with his mop of white hair, he was dancing and singing energetically, "Tin-tin-tin Martyn's lost his last altyn[1]." All his life he had been anxious to live.

I smiled when I kissed his head in the coffin. I gave him a wink, uncertain that anybody would be kind enough to wink at me in my next life. At any rate I didn't say "farewell" to Lazarev.

So we've been laughing and winking at each other ever since. It has become absolutely clear to me now that one's past is the right place for freedom and order—the place where one can arrange everything the way he or she likes. It all depends on one's mood and aims. So Lazarev and I keep smiling, winking at each other, tapping on radiators with pieces of metal, singing, weeping, and going through our rituals. We even try to smile before we run up against this false world unexpectedly and thoughtlessly. For we know what freedom and order are, Lazarev and I. We are idealists.

---

[1] an ancient Russian coin

THANK YOU, DEANNA DURBIN

for Andrey Senatorsky

People in the southern hemisphere seem to be more open-hearted, kind, and intelligent than we. Their mild climate, rich crops, and absolute freedom—in which men may walk around in wide gaudy shorts and women sunbathe in their bikinis on public beaches—yield results. Top this with their industriousness and bewitching smiles and Mother Nature takes care of the rest. If there is happiness on this sinful earth, it's with them—our polar opposites.

With them, everything is different. They have festive holidays and lots of fun; they get together in their small cafes with huge posters on their walls. They forgive their neighbors for their failings and their shortcomings, and you can even find them dancing on the beach. And what about us? At the present moment, just as the laws of opposites require, we drag out our miserable existence, either doing something really boring or waiting in line for food: breakfast-lunch-dinner, breakfast-lunch-dinner, breakfast-lunch. . . . And we have been leading this kind of life for three long months, almost nonstop—for ninety-two days and here's our reward! Here it is!

At least that was what Peter Gorodnyuk, chef of the refrigerator trawler Smyshleny, thought—Peter Gorodnyuk, otherwise known by the strange nickname Deanna Durbin, because of an intriguing tattoo on his arm. The name of this American actress, who in the days of Gorodnyuk's youth was extremely popular in the Soviet Union, stretched in big crooked letters down his strong, tanned forearm.

"I met her when she was on tour in Moscow," he said. Gorodnyuk liked telling his shipmates this secret from his youth, though everybody was already bored with it.

But there were other reasons people on board didn't care much for Gorodnyuk.

Striding fiercely along the deck, refrigerating plant engineer Vitkovsky—chairman of the ship's committee and the people's elected representative—stopped another elected representative of the people, the telegraph operator Malikov, who was able to divine the future of all humankind simply by interpreting the inferences of radio broadcasts.

"Malikov, did you notice something?" Vitkovsky aske in the tones of a Robespierre who had discovered a long-expected conspiracy.

The psychic telegraph operator, ashamed that he might seem uninformed, pricked up his ears and opened his eyes wide. "I did notice something, Comrade Chairman!"

"That's it! The man is utterly insolent. He must think we're stupid brutes. He must want to be put ashore in the next port. He'll get what he deserves." And then he uttered what, for a fisherman, was a terrible oath: "It's not for nothing that I've ruined millions of fish!"

Malikov zealously agreed, while trying to guess who could be so much at fault, and then added, "Yes, that's right. This can't go on any longer."

"Two days on end! For two days this terrible thing has been going on. Why is nobody saying anything? Where is your conscience?"

The telegraph operator nodded, swirling in a sea of conjecture.

Vitkovsky went on fiercely with his case for the prosecution.

"Now, you Comrade Telegraph Operator, what did you eat yesterday?"

Malikov, like many other members of the crew, was not a refined gourmet, nor did he know much about international cuisine.

"Uhh . . . porridge, wasn't it?" he mumbled, feeling deadly tired of this strained conversation.

"Porridge. . . ," Vitkovsky mimicked with a drawl. "For two days the personnel have had to gobble so-called meatballs-à-la-grecque. I've already prepared a telegram to send to the Ministry. It's time to remove our chef."

The Smyshleny's chef had been assigned to the trawler quite recently; his predecessor had been transferred because of illness. As was usual for anyone on this job, he was enormously fat and therefore kind and even sentimental.

In the southern hemisphere, Deanna Durbin suddenly became homesick. Having given instructions to the kitchen boys, he would leave them, bend over the rail and watch the waves stream by with his aging, weak eyes. Pink, yellow, and greenish forests decorated the bottom of the seas, and unbelievably beautiful and ugly fish were hiding there.

Gorodnyuk drank surreptitiously and in moderation. He avoided mingling with his colleagues and, of course, all officials. He carefully discharged his duties; meals were served on time, and they were nutritious and well prepared. His menus were adequately planned. After the ship left any given port, he carefully calculated the rations for each day, keeping in mind whatever provisions were available. But his childlike reveries finally unsettled the old man, and he made a mistake. He altered the menu—two days of meatballs-à-la-grecque. And now his future was hanging by a thread much thinner than a fishing line.

The Smyshleny committee, whose vigilance would be the envy of the security force of any government in the world today, passed a sentence which was severe, but left a tiny hope, no larger than a tropical fish:

"If you dare do it again, we'll make you leave. We'll send you to Novorossyisk, where you'll have to work in some cheap canteen. Go and poison the Greeks there with your meatballs-à-la-grecque. And your salary will be exactly what you deserve: ninety roubles. And then you'll steal, every evening dragging meat from the storehouse. And you'll be living like all the rest. Take the word of a Communist! It's not for nothing that I ruined millions of fish!"

Vetkovsky's words droned in the head of the unfortunate Gorodnyuk, where they merged with the hoarse croaking from Polly, the Madagascar parrot who had been caught God knows when by some sailors and who now commented on everything around him from a big iron cage dangling from the ceiling in the wardroom.

Deanna Durbin left the Comrades' Court feeling as if he were the lowest thing on earth. To say that he was like all the rest! How could they think such a thing!

"It looks just like the insurrection on the battleship Potemkyn," he muttered; "Uhh . . . like in the movie. . . ."

The warning really held a ominous ring. The ship's crew enjoyed one or two privileges that set them above mere mortals. First, there was the opportunity to earn hard currency, which meant they could bring home gifts from overseas for their closest friends and relatives. Then, too, they could purchase jeans and tape recorders to trade on the black market back in the Motherland. For this Gorodnyuk held on to his position as grimly as death. He did work hard. In fact, he was the best in the crew, but now he had to be even better if he were to keep his position.

And meatballs or not, the voyage went on. The Smyshleny, absolutely indifferent to the problems and faults of its cook, floated into the magnificently green Port Jackson Bay, where people so utterly different from us and so deeply loved by Gorodnyuk had founded their first settlement long, long ago. *Sydney*: this was the name of the distant handful of skyscrapers and industrial puffs of smoke that rose up straight ahead.

There are no words to describe the excitement with which a sailor, especially a Soviet sailor, sees a foreign port. Even James Cook, sailing once in this part of the world and drawing up his map of the Australian coast, hardly rejoiced with more passion when he grounded the "Endeavour" in the crack between two reefs. Each ship, one might add, has its own reefs and rocks.

In Sydney, the sailors noted the shape and appearance of two extremely severe, stone-faced customs officers of Japanese origin. Without any delay they moored next to the anchored trawler. Lips firmly pressed in arrogant smiles, they climbed up its Jacob's ladder.

Oh, dreamer, never trust your optimistic imagination! These officers had nothing to do with those friendly people we imagine when we are in the cold and evil towns of our state.

Captain Leikyn, known as the Master, the only intelligent person on board the ship, a man who occasionally enjoyed looking through the *Big Soviet Encyclopedia*, shrank and drooped like the national flag in windless weather when he saw these men. They refused to follow the captain into the cabin where a table had been attractively laid out for lunch with the traditional vodka and caviar and where they could all treat themselves and carry out the formalities. The Japanese got down to business seriously and scrupulously, obviously having decided to turn the Soviet vessel upside down and inside out right down to the last cigarette.

The Master, accompanied by his bevy of assistants, set off to show the samurais around. He showed them the contents of the holds and the refrigerators and made each sailor fill out a customs form honestly and meticulously. By the time the company got to the wardroom, the Master looked like a smuggler caught red-handed. The parrot, rejoicing at such a multinational group, toppled off his perch and addressed the Japanese with a tirade of profanities and obscenities. We can only guess whether the officials caught the meaning of his tirade. But there was no way anyone could miss that disheveled bird, and at the sight of him, one of the Japanese officers became very excited, as if he had finally found material evidence of Soviet crime.

"And why is this, I wonder?" he hissed ominously in English.

"They can't forgive us the Northern Territories," the mate whispered into the captain's ear. But the Master didn't reproach the Japanese in revenge for the last war. The ship was riding at anchor near the Australian shores, which had experienced only one invasion—rabbits. If Russians are still suspicious of Germans, is it so strange that Australians treat all kinds of creatures, even parrots, with distrust? To take offense in such matters would be quite senseless.

"That is a bird. Write it down. Please. A bird!" At the very moment the captain said "bird," the officer of the deck, Zhyltsov, burst into the wardroom looking rather dissehevled and trying, without much success, to suppress some great emotion. The captain gave him a puzzled look, but his bearing returned instantly. He had a grudge against the man as Zhyltsov had broken the captain's revolving chair in the dack house—a chair in which only he, the captain, was allowed to sit.

Few people trusted Zhyltsov since practical jokes were his main and favorite vocation. The high point of his antics had been simulating an earthquake in a city where the fishing trawler had docked six months earlier. Some of the crew together with the navigator had been ashore on leave. Since they didn't have money to buy anything or visit the bars, they decided to play table tennis somewhere out of town. Zhyltsov, who couldn't play anything, preferred to sit around in the sun and tell stories. On that particular day, he talked insistently about the tragedy of Herculaneum and Pompeii, assuring everyone that he had just read in a local newspaper that Vesuvius was expected to erupt again that very day. Nobody took his chatter seriously and Zhyltsov, having given up at last, fell asleep on the sand. But in the evening he came up to the players again, looking extremely alarmed.

"Hey, don't you feel it? It's quaking a little!"

His eyes looked so sincere that everybody hesitated. And when Zhyltsov took a Ping-Pong ball out of his pocket and it began jumping convulsively and rolling around the table all by itself, everybody understood: disaster was certain. The navigator lamented that it was time to go back, escape, rescue the women and children of Naples, and weigh anchor immediately. If they didn't, hot lava would sweep the port and bury their beloved ship.

And strange though it was, the company now believed him and started running around like mad, shouting and crying, until Zhyltsov got tired. All of a sudden he flopped down by the roadside. Flopped down and lit a cigarette. At such a crucial moment!

"Stop! Enough. Let's wait for a bus."

"Why, Zhilets, what are you talking about? People are in trouble. Something awful may be happening! Great losses! Get up!"

"Come on, boys, I'm sorry." He sighed apologetically. "It was a joke."

And the navigator took out his Ping-Pong ball, took apart the two halves that had been glued together, and sitting inside was a big, very energetic grasshopper who jumped out onto the grass the moment it was free.

"I planned it yesterday. I was looking through the encyclopedia, you know, about ancient towns. It was a good idea, I mean joke, wasn't it? Great, I think!"

And so this clever man, wearing an old slicker, suddenly appeared in the doorway of the wardroom, yelling, "Ah-ha!"

Then he noticed the Japanese screwing up their eyes, and the Master, pale as a ghost. "My apologies, Master, but I have something very important to say."

Leaving the captain to explain to the Japanese customs officers what this questionable bird was doing on board, Zhyltsov went out to the deck with the ship's officials, three captain's mates and the chairman of the ship's committee, Vitkovsky, and announced:

"Today, according to radio Sydney, such and such a Communist Party of such and such Soviet Union reports that such and such a faithful son of our such and such Motherland, and such and such twice or thrice Hero of Socialist Labor, passed away and left us like poor orphans in the faraway part of the Pacific. . . . It's the third time this has happened in the recent past," he added. It seemed to the captain's mates that there was at least the shadow of a snicker somewhere in his monotonous voice.

Senior mate Pasunko, a skillful manager and a Communist since 1939, reacted instantly with a decisive warning: "This will be your last joke around here, you idiot. Next time you'll joke with Siberian bears . . . behind barbed wire. They'll teach you there to love the truth."

"But why, comrades? I'm not joking! As if I didn't understand that you don't trifle with things like this! The eruption of Vesuvius is very different from what I'm telling you now."

Fortunately, Malikov, the telegraph operator, came up to the group at that point and confirmed the tragic truth of Zhyltsov's words. The Captain, having gotten rid of the customs officials and hearing about the misfortune, became even more gloomy and began nervously and aimlessly playing with the buttons on his uniform.

"Grief. Ineffable grief has shaken us again. . . ."

There was another man on board who had rarely appeared during the long voyage. Quiet, reserved, keeping to his bed day after day, Andrei Kuzmin seldom had any contact with his colleagues and was in fact on friendly terms with only one person. This was Volodya Sviridov, an engineer who worked on the fishing apparatus. He was also the ship's projectionist. Together Kuzmin and Sviridov had selected ideologically correct movies for the trip, and Sviridov showed them to the crew twice a week. They contained no fighting. No sex. Not even Deanna Durbin singing Russian-Gypsy songs that Gorodnyuk thought were especially for him. The only lively words during these shows came occasionally from the parrot. On show days the bird insisted that his cage be carried closer to the screen . . . whereupon he what reciting obscenities.

That brownnose Kuzmin may have been a mouse, but he was the First Mate's equal just the same. He had made ideology his business, but until now he had not been able to put it to work; this was his day at last. After outlining the political situation in the world and bringing this singular meeting to an end, Kuzmin suggested that they declare deep mourning, cancel all leaves, and not dock in Sydney, the port of an imperialist state, but simply refuel and obtain provisions. And it was for nothing that Zhyltsov and other goof-offs begged Comrade First Mate to let them go ashore for an hour at least.

"We'll do our shopping with sorrow on our faces and only drink Coke and lemonade."

But the ideological sector was inexorable. The sailors' hopes of buying tons of pantyhose for their girlfriends came crashing down, and their throats, dry from prolonged sobriety, trembled at the thought of all the gin that would not be drunk.

Proper mourning activities were soon in full swing. The sailors decided to take the black tarpaulin covers off the searchlights and cut them into mourning ribbons. Soon strange bows and garlands appeared everywhere. The portholes were draped, and the triangular pennant of the U.S.S.R. fishing fleet was joined by a small black flag. In the crew's quarters and in the wardroom, portraits of the leader, who had suffered such an untimely death, were hung for public viewing. This was especially important since not one of the sailors had ever seen a photo of this leader or even his interviews on TV. But the mourning lasted too long. From time to time so-called political reports on home and international events were interrupted by officials trying to recount the myriad biographical facts of the deceased. All day long Chopin's funeral march played over the ship's loudspeakers, accompanied by the baritone of an Arabian journalist.

Kuzmin, as the main ideologist, considered the first day of mourning quite successful and, walking along the decks with the Master, noted the gloomy faces with satisfaction.

"And here we've arranged a krasny ugolok,[1] a place to mourn the deceased, so to speak," he said, inviting the captain into the wardroom.

The Master looked around, nodding approvingly. Suddenly he started, dumbfounded. The cage, slowly swinging in time with the waves, was

---

[1] or "red corner," a place set aside for political events and celebrations.

empty. Its door was wide open. The parrot had disappeared. They stood in silence for some time. And thinking about the implications of this sudden turn of events, they broke into a cold sweat.

"You get one headache, and you can be sure others will follow right behind," Leikyn said, "For Fate, one misfortune is not enough. It thirsts for an international scandal! It wants to do away with us once and for all."

The captain addressed the officers at dinner. He touched upon the death of the leader but devoted the greatest part of his speech to the escape of the irresponsible bird.

"I'm sure, Comrades, that imperialism is responsible for this. Those customs officers, obviously cold warmongers, myrmidons of Japanese imperialism, knowning the loss we have suffered, took advantage of our confusion and devised this monstrous provocation. The West is mocking us. It wants to smother our state with excessive currency fines. But we . . . but we . . . together. . . ."

Here the Master stopped and began running his fingers down his buttons. He simply didn't know how to oppose these insidious intrigues. Moreover, someone had said that the fine would come to about one hundred thousand dollars. To report this to the Naval Ministry, and on the death day of the Leader of All Progressive Humankind, was equal to signing his own discharge papers. Of course he could make the sailors search for the bird, but in the unlikely event that it was still on board, hiding perhaps in the stuffy hold. Leikyn dropped into a chair. He was imagining how the next day he would be demoted and would have to take a job on a tugboat.

At this very moment, the Smyshleny's chef, Peter Gorodnyuk, nick-named Deanna Durbin and so recently censured, barged into the wardroom like a shapeless sack of potatoes, staggered clumsily and knocked down the portrait of the leader from the wall. Everybody realized that he was very drunk. Deanna Durbin mumbled something, addressing first the people, then the portrait on the floor, and finally the empty cage. The sense of tragedy the old man conveyed was enormous. The only thing anyone could make of what he was trying to say was that he and the dead leader had both been born in the same Siberian village and might well have been good friends at some point in a long-forgotten past. He cried that he and he alone was suffering from the death of such a fine leader and that everyone else was a dirty liar. He grabbed them one by one, trying to peer into their eyes.

"Hypocrites! Pharisees!"

Several kitchen boys followed Gorodnyuk into the room and, smiling sheepishly, started arranging plates on the table—plates loaded with spicy, appetizing . . . meatballs-à-la-grecque. The old man, suffering so many troubles, had clearly lost his mind. That very morning he had solemnly promised the ship's committee that he would treat the crew to cabbage pies, perhaps even beef kebob, when they arrived in Sydney.

The events that followed hardly require description.

"He's making fun of us!" yelled the chairman of the ship's committee, Vitkovsky, stamping his feet.

"Yes, making fun of us on such a tragic day!" echoed the telegraph operator Malikov.

"He's sold himself to the Japanese militarists!" wailed the professional informer and cinema operator Volodya Sviridov.

The sailors in the mess room downstairs started grumbling that their girlfriends would never get new pantyhose because of the way the chef was behaving, and the trawler itself trembled with the uproar. All four captain's mates strained through clenched teeth:

" Get out . . ."

And the intelligent Master himself said, "Oh, shit!"

The fate of this childhood friend of the General Secretary of the Communist Party of the U.S.S.R. was quickly sealed. A few minutes later, the command got in touch with the Ministry, the whale boat was lowered, and an absolutely drunk Deanna Durbin was taken ashore, to Sydney, where officials escorted him to the ship Mikhail Sholokhov, bound directly for Vladivostok.

"Soon, very soon, you'll be getting your ninety roubles! And then you can steal, you bastard! Just like everybody else!"

All the next day the Smyshleny, deep in mourning, sat like a black crow at the end of the mooring in Port Jackson Bay. But the oil, fuel, and provisions, all of which had been ordered earlier, were delivered on time.

The only noteworthy incident involved the meat. The second mate, expecting that the ship was going to be fined heavily, decided to buy the cheapest meat he could find. Eventually the Australians delivered a heap of bones, so bare they seemed almost to have been polished. The Master was taken aback: "What do you think we need these for?"

But the butcher obviously didn't care. "How would I know? Maybe you want to start carving bones . . . to express your grief. You Northern People do that kind of thing, don't you?"

"Oh, don't bother me." Leikyn was sick with all the problems and decisions that had to be made about such trifling matters. He was frightened at the thought of the impending return of the customs officers and could think of nothing else.

The fatal hour was fast approaching. Being so terribly upset, Leikyn was ready to excuse even the sins of the navigator Zhyltsov.

Every navigator in the world seems to possess the irritating habit of constantly looking out the window. You can speak to him, confiding your innermost thoughts and feelings, but a navigator responds without even turning his face to you. He keeps looking out the window, looking ahead. Such is his profession! Now came the last day before leaving Sidney and Captain Leikyn, together with his cheerful navigator Zhyltsov were upstairs in the chart room. The Master was sitting on his broken chair, the navigator leaning over the semicircular sill of his inspection window.

"Yes," he said again. "Our parrot's gone and the Kremlin Parrot's gone too."

The captain couldn't engage in such counterrevolutionary talk, of course, but he grumbled amicably, "Oh, stop it, please, will you! Even these walls have ears. Better get prepared for our disgrace!"

"Never mind. But you know I was watching. If rats escape from the ship, it's clear—you'll go down. But what about parrots? What does it mean if they escape?"

The captain got up, looking around wistfully.

"Ah, to hell with you! You clown! Look—the samurai are coming. Now we're in for it!"

The captain's belief that Western intelligence services were concerned about the disappearance of their parrot proved to be true. The moment the

Japanese came aboard, they began insisting on inspecting the wardroom with its empty cage. But the Master insisted that they check the holds first and then look in the lesser rooms. He was especially persistent in showing them the shining, senseless bones. Perhaps he planned to confuse the enemy this way. But sooner or later, he had to take the sinister guests to the wardroom. Imperialism, rejoicing in its forthcoming triumph, was ready to strike its ultimate blow. There was no chance for rescue. The parrot's cage was, of course, empty. Captain Leikyn was prepared to beg for mercy and endure any humiliation.

"Where is the bird!" The question had barely escaped the lips of the heartless officials when suddenly there was a burst of a cheerful noise and laughter. They all turned and saw old Deanna Durbin. The chef stood in the doorway, buried in colorful packages and bags and wearing a ridiculous hat on his bald head. Carrying a hatbox in one hand with the other round the waist of a small, confused prostitute, he was smiling the disarming and happy smile so characteristic of those who live in that part of the world.

"Here's the bird!" he pronounced distinctly. He opened the hatbox and pulled out a large sea gull. The bird was so enormous it could barely have fit in the cage.

The customs officers grew incensed at such barefaced forgery, but the captain, immediately assessing the situation, burst out laughing and poked his finger at the customs declaration where it was clearly written—a bird! And nothing more!

"Here's the bird. Ah-ha!" He was almost sputtering with laughter.

Somewhere behind Gorodnyuk, the crew was jubilant.

"We've got a new bird!"

Enjoying the bright southern sun, the captain's mates, the menacing inquisitor Vitkovsky, the telegraph operator Malikov, and even despicable informer Volodya Sviridov roared with laughter. They behaved exactly like their polar opposites on the far side of the world. They might just as well have danced on the beach, excused the weaknesses and shortcomings of all and, dressed in wide gaudy shorts, found their way along embankments and avenues.

The world of Western democracy, as represented by the Australian shore, gazed in bewilderment at the Soviet ship flying its black pirate flag, ready to capsize with laughter.

And Comrade Kuzmin, the principal ideologist among them, laughed as well, casting glances at Gorodnyuk's girlfriend. He assured himself that the chef had redeemed himself and that the parrot-dissident was certain to propagandize the Soviet way of life deep inside thick capitalist woods. He also imagined that those in the Kremlin had recovered from their recent shock and were now raising their champagne goblets to the resourcefulness of Soviet sailors and proposing toasts to a new leader[1] of our common socialist cause. To a new bird!

---

[1]Namely, Mikhail Gorbachev, general-secretary of the Communist Party of the Soviet Union, who became the first and last president of the U.S.S.R., and during whose term of office the Communist Party was dissolved and the Soviet Union collapsed.

LEGEND OF THE BITTER FROST

"Today not even children—except those small enough
To get a free public bath—believe all that stuff about ghosts,
Or underground kingdoms and rivers, or black frogs croaking
In the waters of Styx, of thousands of dead men ferried
Across by one small skiff."
—Juvenal. Satire 2, 14 9-152, *The Sixteen Satires*,
translated by Peter Green (Penguin, 1974)

"Like a guest that calls, the Christmas star looked in."
—Boris Pasternak, "The Star of Christmas,"
The Poems of Dr. Zhivago, translated by Donald Davie
(Manchester University Press, 1965)

That night in the capital, a star fell;
The bitter cold went up off the scale;
Even deer were crying in the snow,
While peasant dreams of paradise went up in flames.[1]

But the world, always written in prose,
In blissful ignorance continued to grow.

Dark as the final darkness that night
The bar and whorehouse locks went black.
While treacherous, treasonous criminals
Dragged around their heavy chains.

In former times, a phalanx of arrows
Attacked the very same fortress wall.

---

[1]Vladimir Ulyanov (Lenin) died 24 February 1924 , two weeks after the Orthodox Christmas.

In a castle far outside the city were rumors,
The signet ring was in casket with you,
Lying in state, awaiting the laments.
The staff, still thinking of the courier,

Walked around studying the visage,
A face going nowhere soon.

Doctors peered into the hall,
The stains on the mirrors were covered,
But until the news reached Rome,
It was understood nothing had happened.

You could say the loss was a dream
But always in his eyes the look of death.

Everything in turn took on a gloss,
As though the dead and waxy hand
Were glowing with an even greater will,
More imposing than the wet birch trees.

Seeing the powdery snow on the ledge
You could imagine how this brain had perished.

The crowds gathered in the doorways,
Then moved through the house like shadows on sheets,
Pausing by the body like an honor guard,
Trying to imagine the coming week.

Pine needles fell softly on the road.
A meaningless alarm went out.

By around six the next morning,
The unwelcome news had spread.
The gloomy successor idly scratched
The frozen tin plate with nails.

He trailed behind indifferently, the flunky's
Oily flattery smearing the bereft like tar.

The forest itself stayed calm,
Drooping pine boughs trembled.
Only the clear blue blanket of snow
Could summon a burning tear or two.

Peasants would chatter on a passing cart
Crushing the snow as it creaked past the shrine.

But time was in no rush to turn back
Today—better to just go along.
Obedient hands carried the small coffin,
Like a fairy tale treasure past the throng.

You could see the treetops, pillars, viaducts,
Randomly the tunnels lit up.

The capital readied for its awful guests,
Black cloth draped from windows.
Pickaxes clanged against the stony ground,
Frozen right down to its bones.

The cosmos subtly dropped a note that read:
"Don't live too simply this time around."

Everywhere the heavy footsteps of fatigue.
Abandoned by the gaze of the weary crowd,
The corpse set sail along the sobbing waves
Of Cocytus, marking the buoys of its fate.

Huge, despondent granite slabs jostled.
There was no place to put a makeshift pile.

The names of the grieving were legion,
But the memory faded like a dream
Of the days he spent in the smoke-filled temple
Right before the day of the funeral.

Or, looking at it differently
Before he rose again to a beautiful throne.

With unusual arrogance the dead men
Did not rush off to join his ancestors,
But as before and forever hence,
He departed as the victor.

He spurned his indigent petitioners
Without so much as a glance.

More than a religious procession,
He went out in the ferocious frost
Surrounded by banners, wrapped in a shroud,
On the shoulders of friends mad with grief.

On the way to the paved forum,
No one held bouquets of roses.

In the city, the bonfires blazed all day;
People worn out from the great games
Gathered by the fire, knocking their boots
Imagining they'd live to see better times.

Frightened Turkish women, peeking out from
Their veils, took tiny steps in the snow.

Someone else was fighting to first blood
And drooling to take his place under this sun.
To distance of a highway mile
Tested the resolve of those who'd come.

Just a few were blocking the view,
Believing every sorrow to be unique.

Anxious teenagers shut their eyes,
And thereby closed the generation gap.
Under a commander's papal helmet
Glowered a bigshot's ruddy face.

Spit-polished leather shone like anthracite
Taken from a deep mine at night.

This fearless winter reached its peak.
Wreaths even came from the local jail.
It would be hard to call this languid exit
A feast during a time of plague.

Nature herself, no matter what,
Couldn't take back these thoughts.

For exactly here was the Foundation laid.
A few words left when the dust had cleared.
A pathetic group of ambassadors
Couldn't muster a pompous smile.

The call of military violins went out
Above the steam rising above their heads.

The crowd's breath engulfed the zenith.
Shards of ice flew up from hooves.
Passersby remarked in confusion
That new Caesar had not a hint of beard.

Against a backdrop of national mourning
He was undeservedly forgotten for now.

Doubt pounded in his temples.
Processions . . . accolades . . . the grave.
Though he greeted the news coolly,
He didn't approve of this earthly melancholy.

He didn't know what was really happening,
Or who he ought to send troops against.

But he understood who was truly great.
And didn't care he was a mere double.
Besides, to hold on to the eternal power
The connection was important.

In fact, regarding the intransient glory,
One of them held his tongue forever.

For the dead man, deeply mourned,
This country was the best grave around.
While everywhere things were breaking down,
In this part of the world the truth was clear.

If the soul is an illusion, the leaving of the body
Would still be true for all times to come.

While the celebration of imperishability lasted
The status quo was restored in the heavens.
His sarcophagus became an unseen wonder,
Considering itself a higher god.

According to the logic of the Testaments,
The people would have to choose only one.

The small men in their leather clothes,
Who would make any mortal tremble
Embodied this last integrity,
This knowledge that history is just a lie.

Besides, there already was a place
Where you could do exactly as you pleased.

Gun salutes, or an execution?
Beneath the old women's laments
The half-dead expanse of the last Rome
Slowly froze over the Mesozoic chalk.

The new age swept by like a snowstorm,
Carrying away millions in its wake.

Whistles screamed throughout the countryside.
Searchlights at the borders burst into flames.
His troops swore their allegiance again,
Believing the legend of this worthiest of men.

From hunger, or else from bitter frost
Dots of color floated before your eyes.

The words seemed inconceivable,
That daily life would suddenly be all right,
That grieving at the spectacle, as over daily bread,
At some point the empty prayer would win.

And more. A star burned in the frozen sky
Two weeks from Christmas, releasing everyone.

I'll say good-bye to every ship,
and the birds heading south,
and every girl I love:
I'll just have to let them go.

I'm not young or dumb enough
To admit to any guilt.
Autumn leaves fly everywhere,
and cover the whole country.

The wind's lullabies plunge our home
into total darkness.
If they play the wedding march in heaven
You won't hear it in your house.

I don't know who'll stick around forever
But then why the endless road?
There are already cities on earth
Where I can never sleep again.

If I have to, I'll name every date
And every city where I've loved.
It's lucky I can remember that, since
Everything else is gone.

AUTUMN RAINBOW

Streetcars carry stars of electricity on their horns
In Khruschev baroque, the sun glinting on buildings
and coats of arms.
The day's work is done.
It starts getting crowded
Look! a puppy on a leash, rustling in the leaves,
Children's laughter, brightly colored shoes,
(A table overturning in the fruit market?)
Reflected light sparkles in drops of water
Weeds and dirt,
Sleeves rolled up,
Arms, looking for all the world
Like some tangled tree's roots
A sergeant buys a popsicle—it's see-through!
Dusty water. Autumn Rainbow.
In my fingers, I'm holding a green cabbage
But carefully, like a verdant budding brain.

WINTER PARK

Attics fill up like dens with birds.
The train station houses the city life.
Nature, in touch with our magical moans,
Leaves with her head in a blanket of fur.

This means one could slumber again,
If only to end up a Christmas gift.
Any words about completely mysterious things
Must be the names of trees in a city park.

Chalk paths and empty courtyards of summer houses
Are tucked away at night behind ten locks.
Large lanterns moving in circles
Invite someone to dance after all.

The drunken guard patrols the snow
While sticking to the usual diligence of his script,
Protecting the herbarium's faded preciousness
First from Polovetsians, then from Pechenegs.[1]

The icy frames around prickly shrubs,
Shrunk in wool sacking like a monk,
For some ungodly reason translate
Simple phrases into botanical Latin.

Every flower boarded in a wooden box . . .
As though the dead, finding enough strength
To change into real live mourners,
Should sing laments at all these graves.

---

[1]nomadic tribes that repeatedly raided ancient Russia.

THE DELTA[1]

There are such limitless vistas,
Sandy stretches, rivers, archipelagoes,
Big water flowing northward
To where it's desolate, forgotten, unknown.

Sweeping up all the miscellaneous flotsam and jetsam,
Barnacled boats, fishing tackle, old flags, seaweed,
For one thing only—to keep flowing on.

Carrying within it our glances,
the shrill cry of eagles,
Acrid smoke from bonfires.

Looking out upon such water demands candor
I seem to recall this
(tho' was surprised by river's chilly distance)

And if you ask me, Where is home?
I'll answer—"don't know"
If you ask me, What's the path?
I'll answer—"don't know"
(Only scribble my name down on more old scrap paper).

---

[1]the delta of Ob River in western Siberia, one of the largest rivers in the world.

TABOO OF THE CHILDREN'S ROOM

The window is washed for the night.
It turned absolutely freezing.
I can't drink fresh water
or hold round things in my hands.

I have to get used to something else
To white alkali, black gauze,
To fragments of dried cardboard
That's enough about freedom.

No one knows what's more vain
Peace of mind or anxiety.
Cats dream also
of stroking the hair of men.

I'll keep quiet about this too.
Deafness is almost perfect.
Whatever it is you ask for.
All I need is a door.

THE MUSEUM OF NATURAL HISTORY

The museum of natural history in Greenville was solemnly opened about forty-five years ago, and many celebrities and politicians came to the dedication, including several senators (one of whom later became president). At the time, no one could have imagined the deep impact this museum would have on the thinking, the *modus operandi* and *modus vivendi*, of several generations and how it would change, to an extent, the course of history—or natural history, if you wish.

Our region has long been a mecca for archeologists and paleontologists, abounding, as it does, in such an unbelievable variety of finds from all periods and epochs that journalists once suspected we might have been played for fools. The caves in our mountains swarm with paintings, fragments of pottery, and arrowheads, as if they had been used by evolving Homo sapiens as both lodgings and tombs. But most amazingly Greenville appears to be the only place on the continent to show signs of habitation by ancient anthropoids. Until recently, it was thought that our continent had been inhabited only since the Ice Age, since traces of anthropoid apes had never been found here. A nation of immigrants! As if the "natives" had arrived here at some point from God knows where. A land without a past. A land of perfect emptiness. A New World, indeed! And then all of a sudden: the discoveries at Greenville! They came as a shock. It was deeply confusing. Within ten miles of our mountains, the remains of higher primates were discovered in the broadest imaginable extent of their evolutionary development. And if Europe had been proud to possess the bones of two hundred Neanderthal men, the Greenville phenomenon simply confounded Science.

Still more bizarre was the fact that, together with human remains, the area exhibited fossils of even more ancient epochs. Moreover, these fossils were usually in very good condition and were fully consistent with the laws of the geological development of sedimentary rocks. Thus, prehistoric periods were followed by new periods, epochs by new epochs—and nowhere else were excavations so clearly authentic as in Greenville. Coelenterata, Porifera, Chelicerata, Crustacea, mollusks, fish, reptiles, birds—all these remains of bygone animal worlds were scattered in our so-called Noname Mountains, and the only explanation anyone could offer was that this had been where these creatures died. How? Why? Who could say? Time passed, age succeeded age, but for some reason none could grasp, humans and animals continued to prefer to die in the Greenville area—practically in the desert. I should add that over millions of years the climate here changed very little, if at all. One fine day, the sea had simply become land. I may be mistaken, of course, but I wouldn't be the least surprised if history had proceeded exactly like this.

So, for whatever reason, all sorts of creatures had simply chosen to come here, crowd together and cease . . . yes, cease, which is the critical thing to remember, under the circumstances. After all, nobody knows where all those monsters and savages spent the best years of their lives. All we know is that they died in Greenville. I don't know anybody in our city who is proud of this fact. People simply don't care much about where they live and die. As it happens, I visited this region before the museum opened—it was a hot and boring place. I was not in the least impressed by those archeological items—shovels, scrapers, brushes, strange bones, and bits and pieces from which one could have reconstructed hardly anything. All this was soon jumbled up in my mind (and quite possibly in the minds of our scientists) like the aftermath of some weird storm or war, where you cannot say whose leg or arm is whose, and so no monument can be erected to the dead heroes. It was all discordant, ugly. Could these creatures have been so ugly when they were alive, none of them with particular features or character?

But then again, I remain pretty suspicious about all these excavations. Strange as it may seem, I find them as disgusting as the desecration of graves. But the people of Greenville regarded them differently. After all, they could look forward to the construction of a museum. A museum—that's a different matter! And everyone was enthusiastic about the event. The first museum of its kind in the world, a palace of glass at the foot of the Noname Mountains extending right back into the genuine prehistoric caves—like something penetrating into obscurity—a darkness of underground lakes and endless labyrinths. All this, of course, was not there for tourists. The caves and lakes were real, but visitors were not allowed to venture there.

The museum looked at first very much like a huge film studio: the huge scope of it, the special effects, the crowds of visitors. Commercials advertising our institution flooded national television, and only the wealthiest could afford to visit dull old Greenville. Another wonder! Along came ladies and gentlemen, limousines, doormen, fancy restaurants, lectures in outdoor cafes.

All this turned out to serve merely as a hectic prelude to the everyday life of the museum (a second-rate institution by any definition). What I really want to tell you about is the man who opened a new era in the history of all museums, in the history of our town and, quite possibly, the entire world. I want to tell you because very few people know of his actual fate. Even though I don't know little his life, I feel that he became the most significant figure in the spiritual life of his generation.

However, judge for yourself. At that time I possessed only basic, incoherent information from the mass media, which sounded like something that might have been made up, and it was all fairly dated, too. Only recently did the thought strike me that the history of the Noname Mountains could be finally understood through the life of this man. At first I didn't take the newspaper story very seriously. After all, it was the story of a lunatic, a clinically insane person whose dark subconscious was closed to everyone.

That is probably why I so strongly liked Freddy K., with his unbelievably independent approach to life. I doubt he realized what a fearless man he was. He must have been living as if in a dream a dream growing out of that decaying Greenville museum of natural history where he had begun working as a watchman seventeen years earlier. He was a student at that time and needed to earn his living somehow. By that time the museum was slowly dying and was of particular interest only to the few tourists who came to our town for various reasons or, to be more exact, passed through it on their way to more exciting places. There is absolutely no fun in our Greenville—everything is very ordinary and dull. Why would you come here? For the go-go bar, maybe? But the reputation of the museum survived. Out on the highway, stood an exit sign for the Noname Mountains and a sign indicating the gas station and restaurant nearby, so drivers would sometimes stop for a short rest. At this point, the Noname Mountains didn't have any power to attract life—whether to settle down or to die. Nobody wanted to die there anymore. A desert is a desert, and the dinosaurs and mammoths had been the last who were able to enjoy it.

Why am I saying all this? Simply to point out that Freddy K. chose to work here for no other reason except that an opening for a job at the museum had been advertised in newspapers throughout the state. The idea seemed pretty exotic: to live practically in a greenhouse surrounded by dead stones and burning sand. A weird job—guarding *(but from whom?)* bones and cave paintings from bygone epochs. A truly weird job—all the more so because the museum was well equipped with serious electric protection, an alarm system among other things. There was even a great toy, a Time Machine of sorts in which a pilot—or rather the image of a pilot produced with some kind of video mechanism—took you on a tour of the Greenville area as it used to be millions of years ago. You'd sit on the floor of an elevator, frightened and excited, watching that strange and hypnotizing evolution of the Noname Mountains. You'd watch as giants, green and red and horrible, came from God knows where to die in this neighborhood. In the desert, in Greenville caves. Century after century, just like that. . . .

A dying dinosaur (even a cartoon version) is impressive. He doesn't fall down immediately but stands for a long time with his eyes closed as if waiting for the moment when carnivorous mice will eat up his tail, gnaw his legs—and only then does this huge dragon, no longer feeling pain, begin to tilt like a tower whose foundation has been gradually eroded away by the sea. He tilts and there is no pain in his reptilian eyes.

By the way, those extinct creatures had eyes set so far apart on the sides of their outstretched heads that they saw only a very limited picture of the world; they could see anything they liked but not themselves. Nor was there a mirror in the desert through which one could watch its own death. They would fall down like skyscrapers in distant cities from another age, or like churches that had been blown up. And what is amazing is that when these creatures were dying they never howled. It was as if they were made of plasticine, like the models at the museum now. According to the version visitors saw, the dinosaurs died at the entrance to the Greenville caves with a weird feeling of accomplishment, having finished their tiring march across the continent, arriving from different places and then falling one over another, happy that they were all together at last—big, small, herbivorous, or predatory. There seemed to be some threatening omen indicating the point when the energy of everything alive should metamorphose into some other form, passing into space from this particular spot through a single ozone hole. And there was a reunion, a reconciliation, a sort of perfect harmony a couple of months later, when all that common grave turned into a pile of skeletons swarming with worms. Birds wandered amidst that decay catching the worms, sometimes even splashing them about in the water of an occasional puddle; and if a new dying monster frightened the birds and caused them to fly away, it was clear that someday these birds and other mysterious creatures feeding on the carrion would return—although for a very different reason: to die.

Every epoch in that Time Machine, in the elevator taking you down, right down into hell, would end with the specifics of the deaths of animals and half-humans gathered in provincial Greenville. It all seemed very much like a movie, as did the whole saga of the Nomame Mountains. Freddy, after he began working at the museum, could play with that machine without any difficulty. But why would he want to see the same thing over and over? Like watching again and again the collapse of skyscrapers and churches. But then again: the words of psalms are also very monotonous, too. Sometimes it seems that in order to be saved, one need only repeat the same word or endlessly look at the same picture or object for an indefinite amount of time.

One may assume that Freddy didn't care in the least about the destruction of human empires. He was a watchman in the graveyard of a history indifferent to the lives of Augustus and Aristo, Balzac and Buñuel, Chekhov and Churchill, Zeno and Zhukov. . . . In that godforsaken place, in the desert, behind the glass walls of the museum, he was given an opportunity to witness the rise and fall of totally different epochs. There were no countries or states there, no presidents, no nations busy advancing toward the heights of progress. There were only exhibits, stuffed creatures, scenery, everything that makes a game a game. It's no wonder that Freddy got carried away with it.

The museum had very few visitors. The director, taking advantage of its lost popularity, spent his time traveling. The museum was divorced from the world, like Greenville itself, which, to be honest, had always lived in the shadows. Indeed being so completely forgotten and out of the way seemed only natural for both town and museum. Completely so! Freddy, however, felt very uncomfortable at first. He couldn't understand what his position was supposed to be: was he a watchman (as stated in his contract), a warden for those monsters, or a guide to the exhibits spread out under the burning southern sun? He would wander from one hall to another thinking of whether the situation was favorable to his educational ambitions. He already knew the varieties and bones of various animals. He knew in which particular spot of the museum our planet could be viewed as plasma, where it developed into one whole continent surrounded by ocean, where life gleamed in a faintly flicker in submarine masses, and where it came out to the shore. He knew how all those wild animals began to bite, multiply, think. . . . And yet he saw this all as a swarm of worms and dragons that would come to his hometown, to Greenville, to die after being born and spending their lives loving and struggling elsewhere.

Freddy had his own ideas and feelings about Greenville. He knew it like the back of his hand, and he knew the museum like the back of his hand, too. Judging from the phone bills, he called his numerous girlfriends dozens of times a day. I can't, of course, say what they talked about, but I wouldn't be surprised if it went something like: "Did you ever fuck on the back of a diplodocus?" "A what?" the woman would ask. "One of the huge dinosaurs in Gallery Three," Freddy might casually reply.

It looked very much as if he held parties in the museum. Cleaning ladies complained that they sometimes found empty beer cans and bottles in one of the aquariums and that in the morning bikinis and bras hung down from the pterosaur wings suspended from the ceiling. A baseball cap pulled over a stirakosaur's horn almost caused a scandal when a newly elected mayor of Greenville, visiting the dying museum, asked if the prehistoric animals played baseball. He must have been kidding, but Freddy K. got away with it by declaring that the cap had been put there to bridge the epochs and that it was critical to do such things, crude though they might be, to attract more tourists.

Whatever people thought of that explanation, they never considered firing him. Leaving the museum, the director hastily shook Freddy's hand. The director was going to France in a few hours, a pursuit much more fascinating to him than any Neanderthal discoveries. But Freddy, instead of feeling relieved and continuing his fun, immediately then withdrew into himself and gave up his girlfriends. He sort of disappeared, or dissolved, into the museum. Suddenly, he seemed to feel responsible for all that junk, perhaps realizing that he was the only one who could protect it from trespassers. He may even have begun to feel some kind of loyalty to our town. He appeared on local television once and spoke well of the museum's administration. He seemed so well mannered and honest that the Greenville public began to think of him as the museum's real manager. After the television appearance, museum attendance jumped to a few thousand a month. But at this point, for reasons unknown, Freddy completely disappeared from the scene.

He was offered enormous sums of money to go on publicizing the museum, but aside from his guard duties, he simply disappeared. He would sit patiently in his tiny room during the day and roam about the exhibition halls at night, uniformed and armed. Probably it was then that he became interested in paleontology and comparative anatomy. Chances are that the modern theory of evolution didn't exert any impression on him. The accumulation of ancient bones looked like a joke, and had it not been for all the evidence proving the fossils were real, Greenville could have become the joke of the century, compared to which the "Piltdown man" (Eoanthropus Dawsoni) was child's play. Greenville seeme a fantasy, a work of art, an inexplicable freak of nature, and although its existence only confirmed Darwinism, it still resembled a grandiose fake. Of course, no theories could explain why the animals of this vast continent had all come to die in this one specific place. If you can't explain that, theories of evolution look like just so many words. Why was it that our particular continent had only one graveyard throughout its million-year history? Thanks to Greenville, a mystery lay at the heart of the theory of evolution, a mystery that would make anyone wonder. Freddy K. clearly tried to solve the riddle with the help of scientific studies. Afterwards they found in his tiny room the works of Georgius Agricola on mining, Konrad von Gesner, Otto von Guerike, G.L.L. Buffon, and Georges Cuvier, among others—all of them relatively exotic reading for people these days. To all appearances, Freddy never read Lamarck or Darwin, perhaps because he just didn't want to. It is quite possible the books found in his room were borrowed from the museum library and never opened. Freddy, in any case, was guided all his life by his instinct.

Who would have expected that when he began studying the the caves, he would learn how to work stone and bone, make shell ornaments, record the phases of the moon on plates of bone, and cave paintings similar to those of ancient men? The paintings, which portrayed in exact detail weird figures following one another demonstrated great taste. Freddy was not imitative. He didn't damage what he found in the underground grottoes but lived there in his own way. Doing so became more and more important and meaningful for him. But why? His paintings reminded one vaguely of animal images but were actually a meaningless combination of geometric figures. It would be easy to poke fun at his escapades, and let psychiatrists deal with the way a crazy watchman's mind was formed, but you couldn't ignore it. There was something behind Freddy's actions, something very significant and essential for all of us, perhaps even more important than the long history of Greenville. History is always history, something more or less imaginary, and I, for one, cannot be satisfied knowing only that our town was once a graveyard for every living thing. Why had it happened? What was going on in the head of our watchman when he began to dress up in a bearskin and spend night after freezing night next to the wax figures of savages? We know now that sometimes he played sounds over the loudspeakers—imitations of the sounds of ancient woods—and all those extinct protobirds and pangolins would fill the museum with their roaring and clamor and screams. Palm trees and man-made pools together with smells distributed throughout the museum by special air conditioners helped Freddy grow into his role. But it couldn't be contagious, working there, could it? The environment was unnatural, and so was Freddy's bliss among stuffed animals and humans. And yet under the circumstances, it seemed a most natural thing for him to do. Freddy was not playing a game.

Of course, it could have started as a game, and Freddy could have jumped from one tree branch to another, or swung on vines like Tarzan but in his heart begun thinking of all this as very sacred and solemn. Eventually this led him to a wholly different mode of behavior. Submitting or resigning himself to natural forces or technical achievements (of which our museum was the best example), he became an exhibit himself—a weird, useless exhibit that was not part of the displays but that woke up with the first rays of the sun, hurried to his office, put on his security uniform and watched an empty highway very closely and seriously.

I don't know why, but the managers had long suspected something was wrong. Perhaps it was because Freddy had so obviously changed, or perhaps somebody reported the strange cry of a bird late at night out near the Noname Mountain highway, or perhaps . . . . Whatever it was, one day an impressive group of men showed up at the museum. At four in the morning, Freddy, of course, was standing there dressed in his bearskin outfit playing the role of an ancient hunter. He reacted promptly, turned off the sound effects, and let the delegation pass by without noticing anything unusual. Then he rushed back to his little room and appeared promptly before the commission wearing his uniform and looking very proper, all of which only proves that Freddy had certainly not lost all of his senses. His brain, sight, and hearing functioned perfectly, as had no doubt been the case with prehistoric man. He was in his right mind, though to be sure it is well known that insane people can sometimes demonstrate incredible inventiveness and reasoning power.

This sums up almost all I could find in the newspapers. And I could easily finish my story right here, if it were not for the scandals that broke out after Freddy's death. Everything I have told you so far about Freddy K. is more or less trivial. But after the watchman of the museum of natural history died, something more important was discovered. He had not been alone. At least two people had been living and performing strange acts in the museum for two years.

I cannot imagine whether Freddy was terrified, shocked or happy the night he noticed a wax figure rolling its eyes, a figure so familiar that he could never have imagined it as a living being. I wouldn't be surprised, though, if Freddy accepted the "old man" with as much composure as if they had both belonged to the same prehistoric era. He might even have considered all the museum exhibits more or less animate or capable of unexpectedly coming alive, as if they were part of some old movie. I suspect both Freddy and the old man considered their encounter perfectly normal, if not natural. They were two savages, unable to speak, and so had to communicate intuitively in the language of gestures and drawings. They are known to have visited the caves quite often. The routes they took together could be easily traced. Moreover, Freddy's paintings became more and more meaningful. At least three paintings were found of two stooped people, one old, one young, trudging along. By this time, Freddy had completely given up conventional paints. The old man must have known about natural deposits of ocher, whiting, that kind of stuff.

I'll bet that Freddy never asked himself a question that bothers me very much: Where did the other come from? How did it happen that Freddy, who was such an efficient guard, could miss the fact that something had invaded his world? How could he fail to notice anything strange, alien or unnatural? He certainly didn't bring the old man there himself. It seems so unlikely that anyone with a mind as sound as Freddy's could allow himself to become involved in such weird and mysterious actions—actions that unexpectedly began to mean so much to him.

It seems most likely that the old man came from the caves. In the life of every Robinson there should be a Friday; it doesn't always work out this way, of course, but it's what we hope will happen. In any case, the old man, this faithful man Friday, proved himself loyal after the death of his friend. Freddy died accidentally, foolishly and a little too symbolically, considering the fate he had chosen. The museum, as I mentioned earlier, was decaying, falling apart, and near the caves there was something wrong with the electric wires. Our Cro-Magnon (I call him that since Cro-Magnons were not as ugly as Neanderthals) died urinating on a bare high-voltage cable. Only after his body, barely covered by necklaces and rags, was found did it become clear what he had been doing in the museum. Death, according to the paramedics, was instant and occurred just twenty minutes before the museum opened. Perhaps that was why the old man didn't react as one might have expected: burying or burning the body of his comrade. There simply hadn't been time.

Can you imagine the old man's despair when Robinson's dead body—the body of his friend, his master—was put on a stretcher by strangers in white linen gowns and taken away in a white squealing car. . . .

The old man dug Freddy up the following night. It's incredible that he was able to find the grave in a cemetery so distant from the museum. It was obvious that the grave had been dug up by hand, as traces of long human fingernails were found in the clay. This caused a real panic, as I learned from the newspaper article. It turned out that Freddy's father and mother and sister were still alive, and they were absolutely shocked.

The old man, God knows why, brought Freddy's body back to the museum, changed his clothes, coated the corpse with red paint and covered it high with clay in the very room in which they had first met. In the process, Freddy's tuxedo disappeared, and of course, his aged parents couldn't afford another in which to bury their son, although they repeatedly returned his body to the cemetery, where it belonged. But the old man dug it up again every time. The scandal got worse.

The first time the body was discovered by visitors on the morning tour, attendance at the museum fell dramatically. After it happened the second time, guards were posted both at the cemetery and museum, but Freddy's man Friday somehow managed to steal the body again. This time he placed it in another exhibit hall, and performed the rituals, so important and critical to both Freddy and himself, and luckily escaped a bullet. It seemed as if life itself were drawing him to some inevitable conclusion. He escaped, leaving traces of blood on the stairs. The police were amazed how easily he had tricked them, standing in one of the exhibits among the animals like a mannequin in a hunter's outfit.

Just ten days later at another cemetery he dug Freddy up again, for the last time, in broad daylight. I don't know how he managed to carry his burden through the town (a total of twenty miles, or thirty-five if he took the roundabout way), but this time he transported Freddy to the caves. Alas, armed guards were still there, and I am afraid they riddled both of them with bullets. Yet the savage escaped again, vanished into thin air and the darkness of the Noname caves. But he was going there to die anyway. He was going to bury his friend where for millions of years every living thing, led by some strange instinct, had gathered to die.

And if we've lost this instinct, like many other gifts we've lost, it doesn't mean that nature is any more simple than it used to be. We can say that the purpose of Freddy's life was to bridge or link epochs—and thus to nullify all the changes brought about by civilization. Doesn't the museum exist to maintain the connection between eras? And don't you think Freddy K. turned out to be an ideal museum attendant? He died where animals and people have been dying for centuries, and I consider him and his friend to be true—or, if you like, natural—heroes. Sometimes I think it was a good idea to establish a museum of natural history here, expensive though it was, for it has the capacity to become a symbol of our power, if we still want to survive.

ALGAE

in memory of Evgeny Peltsman, my friend Harry

Riverside purple rose willows, decay and scum of ditches, derangedly flooded in early April, the tensely droning cores of their cracked branches echoing the peal of the train and rails.

Submerged, tangled forest, a stiff fishnet of thickets, become conscious in water, with the fascination of objects on the keel of a submerged vessel, acclimates itself to chomping its long shadows unwilling to budge an inch.

Perhaps at twilight, concealed with a pellicle akin to goose skin, he condenses into a similitude of warmth, an animated fog from within which faint voices issue into sound.

Colorless, icecold hema from rents in stems coagulates densely on the death-ruptured fibers—animal blood is more frenetic, it never congeals in the form of tongues on the coarse flanks of the spurting stampede.

Staring at war, which is aware neither of tears nor of swoons, not even of the railroad's rumble, just the hubbub of the good world, we are too dim to discern that contentment is the essence of nirvana.

Night's aggregate familiar to the occular sensor, the utterly, simply conscious disintegration of his unperished soul from the nethermost astral strata signifies, in itself, the mustering up of life, the alms of suicides, and the tendencies of the criminal world.

Gulls tread the loam, gobbling up the soaked bread (last year's, like the snow in the proverb),—a coal-green color. A split-second, triangular blade of light slices the wide, shimmering river framed by trunks in a clearcut.

All the same, one notices neither waves nor raw-boned palisades that seen from afar resemble a slagheap; one bank always sloping, the opposite never steep—this, a fact, based on personal observation at these latitudes.

Explanations are always necessary, even in a dream if I meet a man, once dead, I tell him—You can't be here. Your Mom said you're dead. And he, to smooth things over—Don't let this likeness fool you. I am his brother.

There are connoisseurs of dreams and those averse—don't know to which I belong, failing to differentiate between imaginary and real; and this consists neither in boasting nor good fortune, nor in other utilitarian, workaday miracles.

Swampweed trampled in the jaws of a bulldozer's rut, plowed up soil, not a pennyworth's of humus, just a whiff of spring floods, leached out minerals, their crystal lattices left behind like the skeletons of meandering pike fish.

Have you seen the torso of a snake pregnant with a man or with an English key? Or simply a bared sole with a turtle tattoo? Have you heard the speech of the Egregors that may become commingled with coarse Tartar curses?

Highly unlikely that anyone glances much at their feet, at this muddy withered turf. . . And a slob of a snowdrift starts flaring up, a light the whiteness of graveyard phosphorus; and the thicket strips its greasy hands of their gloves.

In the flash of the river one is reminded of the extinction rate of other planets and the forgetfulness of souls that reinfuse you for a second, but you do not notice, you only see some locus on a map. Near water.

There are other planets; it's about time we recognize this in expectation of the heart's full expansion, its animal scream, which, it must be, may be understood only by bats and echo locators—by those that understand graveyard noises and ultrasound.

There again goes the train, constraining the nature of all enervation, in whose progress one can distinguish several notes capable of salvation, or emotion. . . Or of a rap on the knuckles.

It stinks of boot polish, of styling gel, and smoke that wafts over from the conflagration in the reeds; the reeds here flame up every Sunday, one need only drop one's matches skillfully or, for the sake of purity of purpose, set it right on fire.

Spring becomes apparent, like confidence; such bragging oozes forth each season, every April; it resembles complacency, a cavalier manner; my stride is overly impudent, I'm much too certain of myself—not for long, but I am ashamed.

You worked for emergency medical services, a jovial fellow—and when we needed a lift somewhere you would make a call and pose as the husband of a woman in labor, elaborating the most horrific symptoms, for you knew the words uttered in such crises. Of course they'd show up, and of course we'd get a ride back to town. "Man, you really made that up? No one croaked?" "You owe us a bottle for the cab ride." "Yes, I do." "So you set it all up?" "I don't know, don't know, but if someone was giving birth you'd be handy."

You dug picking up "corpuscles," dead men, the ne'er-do-wells, the nobodies, emerging from under the snow, their stiff hands and kissers still striving greedily to grab at something.

Drums of corroded wire, crumbling masonry, because they are only pieces and not construction materials, chunks of rubbish resting on the cadavers' faces, and, still standing, the saberlike reeds, protrude into the sky.

Even if I decide I haven't learned a thing, I am lost to the future; and this sense of indirection is to me more significant than the chomping of dirty water at the heels of my boots, this confidence come to nothing.

For some reason we hike up here and never scramble down the ravine, to the expanse in that depressing ditch spreading its tangle of willows towards the river called Tom'. I was born there also.

The Tom' is significantly shorter than the Ob'. Its source is in the Altai, somewhere in the mountains. It may be easier to learn the language of the Eustinians than that of the Egregors. It is likely also some kind of dialect.

Expectations of life, every year looking forward to life. And the ice floe. In these backwoods one grows accustomed to waiting, if to nothing else. This is harmful to such an extent that after your funeral and the week-long binges (to make the ground soft as goose down) the souls clamber back in various guises, either as dry lightning or as a brother's likeness in some weird old dream.

Is this really the reason I recalled the willows? Riverbank marshes at the feet of the hilltop city. Lost one winter, the Yale key to your glamorous shack. Search and you'll find it. 'Cause I found the button from my raincoat, returning a few days later, along the same road from a visit. After your wedding, buddy. Had I lost the ring I'd have found it likewise.

The dead, they say, are compelled toward fire, and beat a path to it without first divining where they go. They must part all expectation and, as if through a thicket, head straight for the flames, as senseless as it may sound. Because to linger on the shore in the realm of the living would be much too cozy, too easy—cowardly, perhaps even.

Unlikely that even once in our lifetime we had set an heroic example in our youth or childhood. Generally, they whipped us. A few years later the mugs of those dregs bring on a smile—even now I don't pity them; still the same scum as always. Their place is exactly where they find it. No one cares about a bloodied nose, or one's last pennies snatched away for a bottle; it's one's cowardice that's upsetting. It's of no matter any longer.

One's behavior in dreams is a mystery. Who dashes where after the final attack on one's reflection in the mirror or in the palm of the father. We are facing a war that knows neither tears nor motions, and it doesn't even make sense to thrust one's chest in the path of a bullet, because what really counts is the maturity of the soul and not heroism. What in life has already steeped under your skin. Say, for example, not a glow but a radiant birthmark.

We approached cemeteries with levity, for some reason no feelings of awe or repentance were evoked there; burial grounds were a comforting place, especially since it was you who showed me at the local one the lot of the Jews; showed it with a sort of bravado, I don't think intending to lay your body down there.

There are people that traverse borders without passports; there are people, like yourself, who were born and died in the Beatles epoch, there are people, but fortunately beside people there are souls, because the stones of molecular bonds are the ineluctable direction of protoplasm towards organic matter, algae, seaweed, that strange property of mortality for the sake of motion—much too much like life.

A paiper-mâché head from the children's fairy tale—if anyone comes here it will be prince valiant; an evergreen pine by your grave; if anyone comes here, it is just in remembrance.

No one loves marshes and forsaken ditches; indeed no one, beside us, loves graveyards either—but in the water there still swarms the spawn of amphibians, serene and worthy as any century's vermin—I sense that I consist of just such ova, that I am on horseback, a lover until I crumble into a myriad pieces, definitely damp and miniscule.

It is something that gawks with its thousand gaping eyeballs at the sky only, something scattered and silent, some prehistory, protolife, a prologue—and not the trepidation for the soul of a friend departed. It will somehow be settled, what to do now, what path to follow.

The cheap ooze of our recent trust in something feminine. We will somehow resolve what to do without them; they will somehow determine to take some action. Now you, to my woe, are my closest conversant. I wish to speak with no one, except you.

I sense hollowness and treachery in every soul, even if it does slightly resemble a lady—you always treated them with boots, a cavalier attitude, you were often right, even when having cold feet to strike them, but the act must be completed.

Such a regal strike at the porcelain nuptials, at the sobbing from the dungeons, at all the poor people, who never come to admire the "trains," "planes," "the vanishing cities. . ."

The blood of animals is much braver, much more naive—may there again be an interesting production at the drama theater; the herds migrating south, the eagles watering at the rivers. . . Such are the sensations of absolutely unfettered children.

These are only the feelings of a man in the midst of an April depression, swamped by dirty water and my emptiness—with my complete absence in these native places, where we once drank port and bragged about the vigor of our pointless actions. Once again you did the deed, and again before me.

The word "deed" was once mentioned when you flirted with marriage. It still sounds that way, but it turned into drinking; and then I saw in a dream that same hillock, the very thing, alas, that did happen. I am ready for something like this. For my dream brother.

Let's quit our rivalry and chirrup like inebriated birds about the future's rainbow feathers. It's some twenty years since you and I became acquainted—it is shameful to admit now what we know about each other, if we meet in memory by the futile waters.

I hope that by now you would also spit upon the obstinate details of our gorgeous actions. I hope we are still together, and closer still. That we are trudging along the shore in the buzz of the fireflies, that we are rambling, flowing back and forth from evening to morning, that we are entirely senseless—which of us is still here and which beyond already.

That we meander . . .

That . . .

Help me, pal of mine, wherever you may be—if I don't betray you, please treat me likewise. And this is not a ceasefire, it is peace already.

And this has come to only a prologue in expectation of a glimmer from my beloved river. A forelife in expectation of life. Duckweed, algae, fermenting silt. It has turned into confidence, into certainty that we will see the opposite shore. Indubitably, that in the future we will converse. And I mean tete-a-tete. Of course without holding back. In any language. Even in Morse code. Or have you already learned the language of fallen angels? A difficult tongue?

A GUEST IN THE HOMELAND

I'll spill ink, forget to find paper
Because time passes, only exterior
And the spine of the archipelago of the long river
Covers itself with frost in the hesitant dawn.
And bonfires gradually losing their color,
Reflecting each other, remain on the fishing wharf,
Between the grass and suddenly wandering river,
Missing familiar lights at the top of the hill.
Where it's never too late,
To build some stonewall house or some wooden temple,
Only to have to ask yourself again and again,
Why do the floorboards always creak under your feet?
Why does the temple avoid the straight glance
And its tall shadow fall into empty waters?
Man is made up of water, and there's only one respite
That it's possible to capture a fresh breath of freedom,
That you don't need to blaze a trail
From Varangians[1] to Greeks,
Paying special attention to the West or East,
You died a natural death, and in this century.
And so, you are somewhere close by.
And the doors are slamming in my great Siberia.
Everyone's gone. So, soon their souls will go.
Consider them, so that they can easily forget
Man is made up of water, and a ribbon of land.

---

[1]Russian name for the Vikings. "The way from the Varangians to the Greeks" is a proverbial expression with obvious symbolic meaning for Russians.

Vladimir Gandelsman

from AN INTERVIEW WITH VADIM MESYATS

Vladimir Gandelsman: Would you mind reciting something that you wrote, something you really like yourself.
Vadim Mesyats: How about "A Norwegian Fairy-Tale"?

These are not tears—he's lost his eyes.
They rolled into the gloomy wood of Hevald.
A Troll picked them up.
And looked at the Moon.
This isn't a frog—he's lost his tongue,
It sprang into the gloomy wood of Hevald.
A Troll picked it up,
Looked at the Moon and declared, "Moon,
You are more precious than an ant of gold
And rounder than a mossy stone in the swamp!"
He laughed and laughed.
A patrol picked him up.
If you don't want to start crying, try falling asleep.

(*translated by Vadim Mesyats and Samuel Kent*)

You like it?
VG: In general—yes, in particular—I don't think I understand it all.
VM: It's a childlike poem, of course, and related to a children's book that was read to me long ago—*Crows-Utrest* I lost it somewhere, unfortunately. Those were the tales about trolls, the forest of Hevald, and all such things, and it sounded so mysterious, so strange in Siberia. Words like these stick in your memory forever, and when you are crying, you don't really care what

words you mumble. It's just intonation, inhale-exhale. I've always wanted to cry with "strange" unfamiliar words, so that no one could see the particulars—though now I realize how improper it is to be too exotic. I personally think this is a very understandable poem—that's exactly why it was translated. I am afraid that what I consider the best cannot, and should not, be translated. Enough of literary absurdities.

VG: OK. Then let's get to mundane absurdities. How do you like it here in America?

VM: "Real estate doesn't excite me . . . ," Kurt Vonnegut's joke. But seriously, . . . America is a new experience, new life for me, sometimes better, and sometimes worse than what I had before. First of all, America means independence to me, "isolation" from other people, though I don't think I could say what that exactly means. For example, it turned out very important that I learned how to drive and have driven all over the States. This is a completely new degree of freedom: in Russia you won't even find a more or less decent service. My answer may sound very narrow-minded (primitive), but the opportunity to travel is what I consider the main advantage here in America. The opportunity "to pass by." And as for the "isolation," . . . I prefer it to our Russian "fraternization," or rather undue familiarity. At least you know what to expect from anyone. With us, it's either he loves you forever or cuts your throat. But still, it was pretty difficult to get used to many things here. At least Americans don't care what habits and ways you have. I think Europe imposes its "modus vivendi" on the people, in Germany it's always German way, in Italy—Italian, and so on. Here in the States, everything is much easier.

VG: Now about the freedom in the literary sense: Do you have a reader in mind when you write? In other words, do you feel free, do you think the freedom from the reader is really freedom? Is it possible and necessary to control the "irrational" that tends to flow into the "darkness," or simply "delirium"?

VM: It is the irrational level where you have the reader in mind. More important is when you know yourself what you write about. You know, I have a feeling that there is something I simply must write. If not today, then tomorrow—but must, by all means. That is, all these things exist already before they become a reality, they simply bide their time. Of course, it is impossible to think about the reader in this situation. But I am human myself, and write for people, and expect a reaction or response, after all. But as for the "delirium" . . . To complicate poetry intentionally is unfair and indecent. Life is confusing and full of darkness as it is,—what I would want to do is to understand, explain, or at least record it. That is all.

VG: What is poetry to you, in general? Don't you think that a talent is nothing more than a desire and ability to attract attention, to want to be liked, and is beside the point?

VM: First of all, I try to avoid this "talent" notion. If you do write something you have to be talented, otherwise it doesn't make any sense. The desire to attract attention, to want to be liked and admired is a wonderful thing, and the best is to be liked by yourself. But self-expression leads to things like . . . "look how gentle and subtle I am" . . . so I always try to avoid it, to get "dissolved" in something, be it speech or emotions. This is an almost primeval feeling and hardly attainable for a modern human being who is too individualistic. I hope I have managed to "get beyond" the literary limits a couple of times . . . Short stories are a more unimaginative "thing," there are more stylizations there than in poetry.

VG: You have two books of poetry and two prose books published. That's a lot and impressive, given your age. Do you know that Annensky's brother recommended that he not publish poetry until he turned thirty?[1] Didn't you ever want to buy the whole printing of any of your books so that nobody could read it ?

VM: No, never. But again, I never had a brother either . . .

VG: OK, tell us about your strongest artistic impression or incentive or one of them . . . .

VM: I 've had too many impressions, but at some point I realized that non-artistic incentives are much more important to me. Be it dreams, childhood memories, even changes of the weather that, for whatever reason, you remember for the rest of your life. At thirty, I, for example, realized that turtles, or rather the image of a turtle, had haunted me all my life. This image, of course, carries both the mythological and symbolic load—the most ancient reptile, and longevity, and hardiness. . . . But I was astonished by this creature back in my childhood; I was about four years old when I first saw

---

[1]Innokenty Annensky (1896-1909), Russian symbolist poet.

a turtle in the aquarium in Sevastopol, and I remember that my parents only managed to get me out of there by some trick. I can still see her swimming, moving her flippers, opening her mouth wide, her neck all wrinkled. . . . This is love and horror at the same time. They say back then I was even writing letters to her. Well, I can talk about turtles forever, still not knowing how to explain all this love and admiration. . . . By the way I like the fact that their brain volume is so small. . . .

VG: Are we being jealous here?

VM: Sometimes. That's foolish (any jealousy is foolish, though). It's amazing that a thirty-kilogram turtle has a three-fourth gram brain, and some of them can move around headless for days. One experimental specimen (specimen, what a disgusting word!) lived for six months after its brain was removed. They can do without food for years. . . . And still, their life is full of content and beauty. Take their love and attachment to their home . . . They travel all over the world, all seas and oceans, but always lay eggs on their native sandbank; the pregnancy of some of them lasts for three years, and then girls hatch from the eggs left in the sun, and boys from those in the shade. And all those tragedies when these little baby-turtles want to get to the water—they crawl and crawl and everyone tries to gobble them: birds, jackals and whoever . . . I am not an expert in chelonology, but I have my own experience, which is important. A few times fishing in South Carolina I saw turtles catching the hook with their flippers, but when one of them swallowed it, my friend and I tried for an hour to get it out of her mouth, looking into her bloodstained eyes. . . . Anyway, we failed and simply let her go (I hope she didn't die), and later, on the way home, the front tire went flat at full speed. . . . By the way, for about a year now, I've been reading and rereading Steven Hawking's *A Brief History of Time: From the Big Bang to Black Holes*. Here not only incredible facts are important, but rather the compliment to the human intellect. The real things are always more interesting. And, of course, no dreamer could ever think of such a picture of the universe.

VG: A turtle will be one of the main characters in your next novel, right?

VM: Let's not discuss it for now.

VG: OK, let's then get down to earth . . . or rather, crawl out to earth from all those depths—what do you do in that college of yours?

VM: Three years ago I met Ed Foster, American poet and publisher, who teaches at Stevens. We came up with the idea of a Russian-American program, then found some patrons. So, this is basically a private initiative of two people. We've been arranging literary readings, exhibitions, concerts, translations, publications, trips to Russia for Americans and to America for Russians.

VG: Do you really believe that these two poetries can have any "mutual understanding" at all?

VM: If I didn't it believe at all, I wouldn't be doing anything. Though, my initial enthusiasm is gradually running out. At first, I wanted to understand everything, not to make hasty conclusions. Now I get annoyed more and more often, especially when dealing with the translators. Of course, it is impossible to explain certain things: our poetries have different histories and different tasks. I think those American poets that came to our readings try to be too honest. Excessive honesty and adequacy, you know—if you want to say something, just say it—a metaphor has become something shameful. I can't say I myself admire excessive imagery, but there are so many things that still "work" in the Russian language but not anymore in English. I always remember those endless discussions with a very fine poet who works in English and who was translating a poem of my friend Arkadii Zastyrets. From the viewpoint of the Russian language it was "much ado about nothing." There were such lines in the poem:"When the moon blows up its glowing gills, ready to turn . . . " And the translator asks—how come the moon has gills, it's not a fish; that sounds stupid. I answer that this is a "passing prettiness" in the ironic poem, but the membrane that fish has above its gills is also round like the moon, and some fishes can be almost round too. And the translator says: who cares about these "passing prettinesses"? And translates: "When the full moon is slowly swimming across the sky." I am afraid that dispute was not accidental but rather ideological. That is, as one of my friends put it, such "paths" are simply forbidden in the American poetry—too elaborate. For us, on the other hand, these things sound quite normal. I can't imagine how they comprehend, for example, late Mandelstam in the English translations? That is way more serious and difficult than the moon-fish stuff. . . .

VG: Could you comment on a passage from one of your stories? Maybe that will explain something. "But why is revelation supposed to be the perfect bliss? Why is it accepted not to trust anything really indifferent, as if there is nothing behind it except death? Everything living feels it must rush about, strive for the like, reject, and return again. But is this senseless passion, desperate search, which is nothing but doubt, that notorious 'labor of the soul' which should protect us from featureless denial? Everyone knows that we fuss around for each other. Maybe each person, if he joins the surrounding life, which is strangely unfit for him, has then very little left of his own life."

VM: I don't know what to comment on, or explain here. Though I wrote this story about eight years ago, my mood or frame of mind now is the same. Since no one can help you anyway, go ahead and finally decide what you consider most essential and fundamental in yourself, and live relying on it.

Designed by
Samuel Retsov

Text: 11pt Bembo

acid-free paper

Printed by
McNaughton & Gunn, Inc.